STONE ARCH BOOKS
a capstone imprint

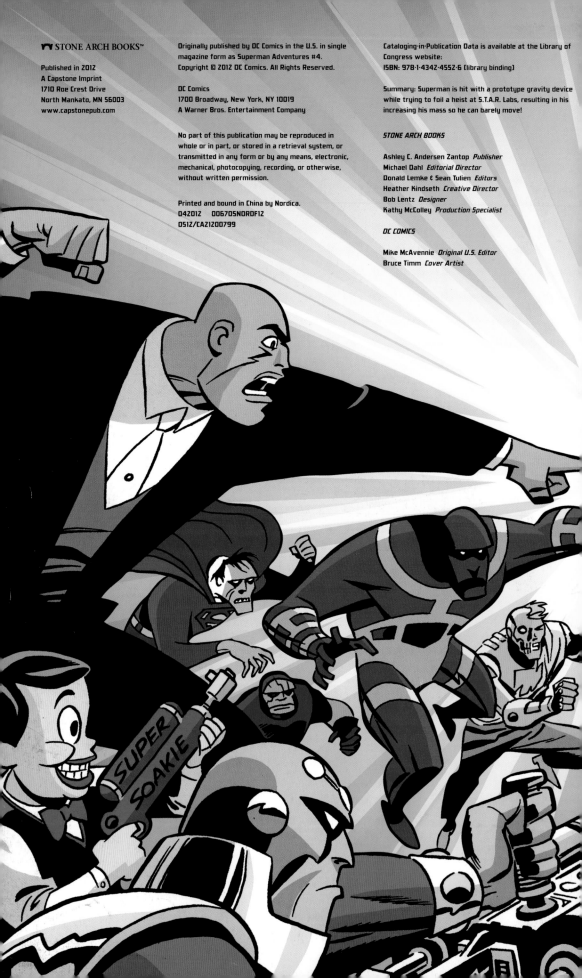

STONE ARCH BOOKS™

Published in 2012
A Capstone Imprint
1710 Roe Crest Drive
North Mankato, MN 56003
www.capstonepub.com

Originally published by DC Comics in the U.S. in single magazine form as Superman Adventures #4.

DC Comics
1700 Broadway, New York, NY 10019
A Warner Bros. Entertainment Company

Printed and bound in China by Nordica.
042012 006705NORDF12
0512/CA21200799

Cataloging-in-Publication Data is available at the Library of Congress website:
ISBN: 978-1-4342-4552-6 (library binding)

Summary: Superman is hit with a prototype gravity device while trying to foil a heist at S.T.A.R. Labs, resulting in his increasing his mass so he can barely move!

STONE ARCH BOOKS

Ashley C. Andersen Zantop *Publisher*
Michael Dahl *Editorial Director*
Donald Lemke & Sean Tulien *Editors*
Heather Kindseth *Creative Director*
Bob Lentz *Designer*
Kathy McColley *Production Specialist*

DC COMICS

Mike McAvennie *Original U.S. Editor*
Bruce Timm *Cover Artist*

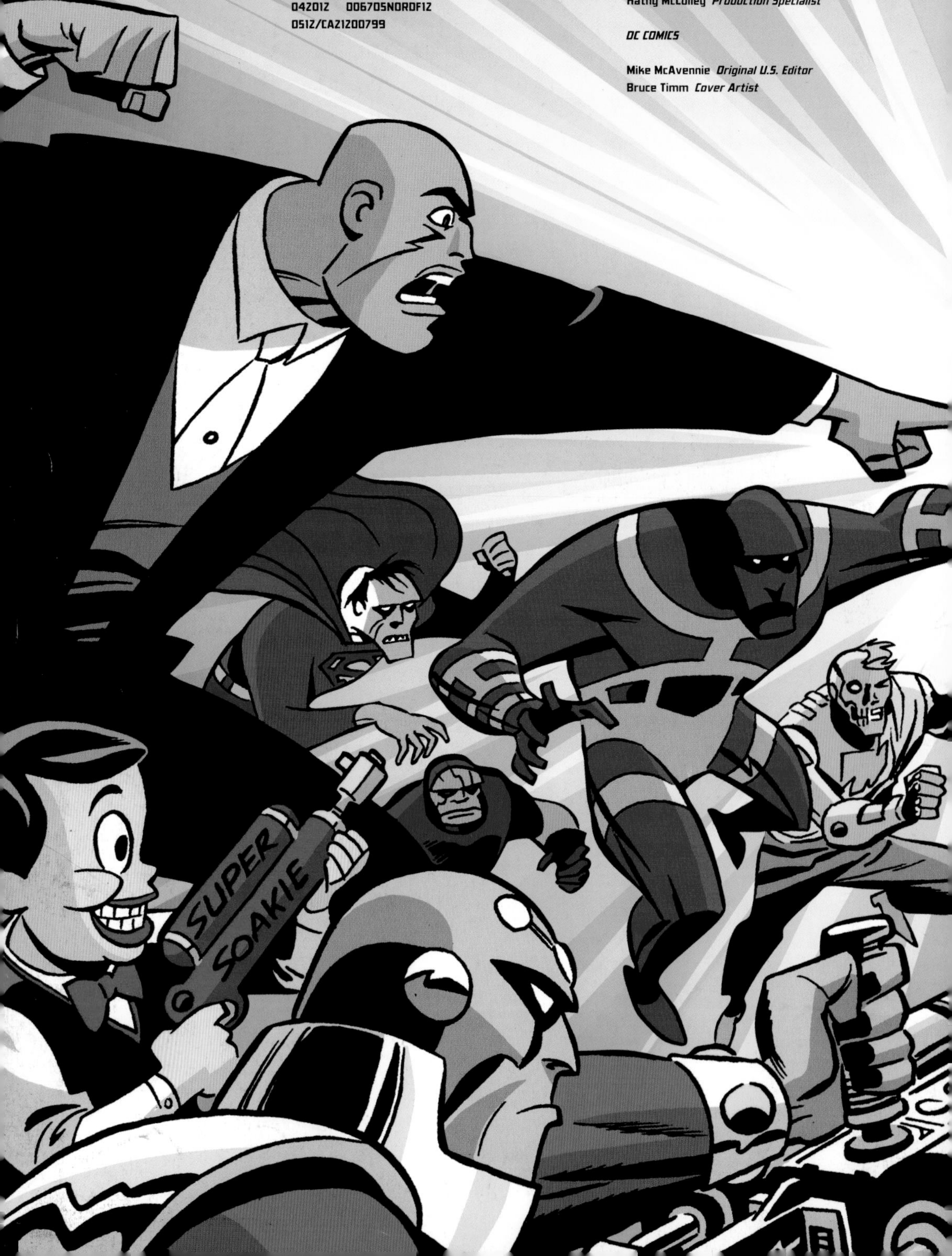
SUPER SOAKIE

SUPERMAN ADVENTURES

Eye to Eye

Scott McCloud .... writer
Rick Burchett ....penciller
Terry Austin .... inker
Marie Severin .... colorist
Lois Buhalis....................... letterer

Superman created by
Jerry Siegel & Joe Shuster

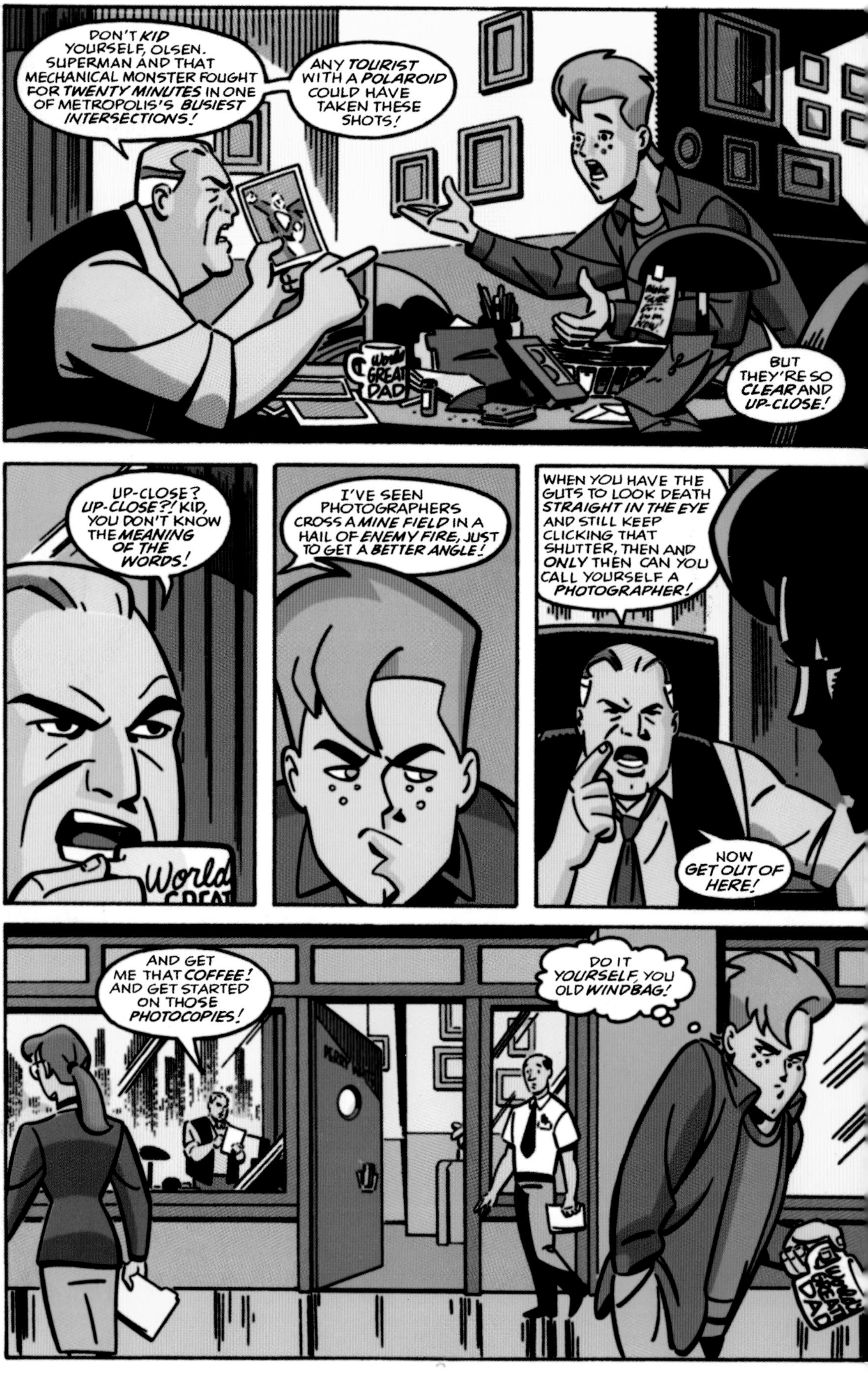
DON'T KID YOURSELF, OLSEN. SUPERMAN AND THAT MECHANICAL MONSTER FOUGHT FOR TWENTY MINUTES IN ONE OF METROPOLIS'S BUSIEST INTERSECTIONS!
ANY TOURIST WITH A POLAROID COULD HAVE TAKEN THESE SHOTS!
BUT THEY'RE SO CLEAR AND UP-CLOSE!
World's GREAT DAD
UP-CLOSE? UP-CLOSE?! KID, YOU DON'T KNOW THE MEANING OF THE WORDS!
I'VE SEEN PHOTOGRAPHERS CROSS A MINE FIELD IN A HAIL OF ENEMY FIRE, JUST TO GET A BETTER ANGLE!
WHEN YOU HAVE THE GUTS TO LOOK DEATH STRAIGHT IN THE EYE AND STILL KEEP CLICKING THAT SHUTTER, THEN AND ONLY THEN CAN YOU CALL YOURSELF A PHOTOGRAPHER!
NOW GET OUT OF HERE!
AND GET ME THAT COFFEE! AND GET STARTED ON THOSE PHOTOCOPIES!
DO IT YOURSELF, YOU OLD WINDBAG!

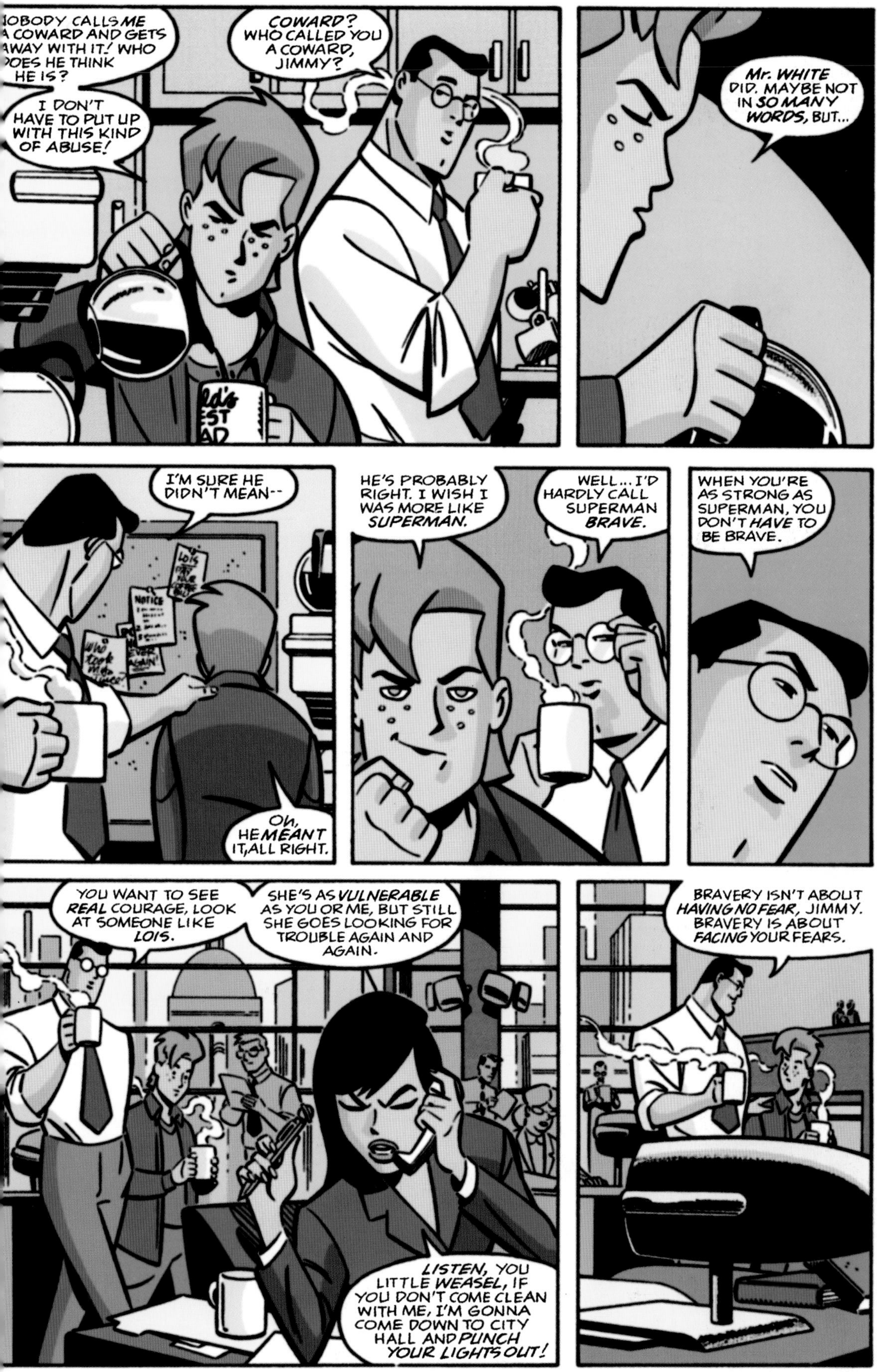
NOBODY CALLS ME A COWARD AND GETS AWAY WITH IT! WHO DOES HE THINK HE IS?
I DON'T HAVE TO PUT UP WITH THIS KIND OF ABUSE!
COWARD? WHO CALLED YOU A COWARD, JIMMY?
Mr. WHITE DID. MAYBE NOT IN SO MANY WORDS, BUT...
I'M SURE HE DIDN'T MEAN--
Oh, HE MEANT IT, ALL RIGHT.
HE'S PROBABLY RIGHT. I WISH I WAS MORE LIKE SUPERMAN.
WELL... I'D HARDLY CALL SUPERMAN BRAVE.
WHEN YOU'RE AS STRONG AS SUPERMAN, YOU DON'T HAVE TO BE BRAVE.
YOU WANT TO SEE REAL COURAGE, LOOK AT SOMEONE LIKE LOIS.
SHE'S AS VULNERABLE AS YOU OR ME, BUT STILL SHE GOES LOOKING FOR TROUBLE AGAIN AND AGAIN.
LISTEN, YOU LITTLE WEASEL, IF YOU DON'T COME CLEAN WITH ME, I'M GONNA COME DOWN TO CITY HALL AND PUNCH YOUR LIGHTS OUT!
BRAVERY ISN'T ABOUT HAVING NO FEAR, JIMMY. BRAVERY IS ABOUT FACING YOUR FEARS.

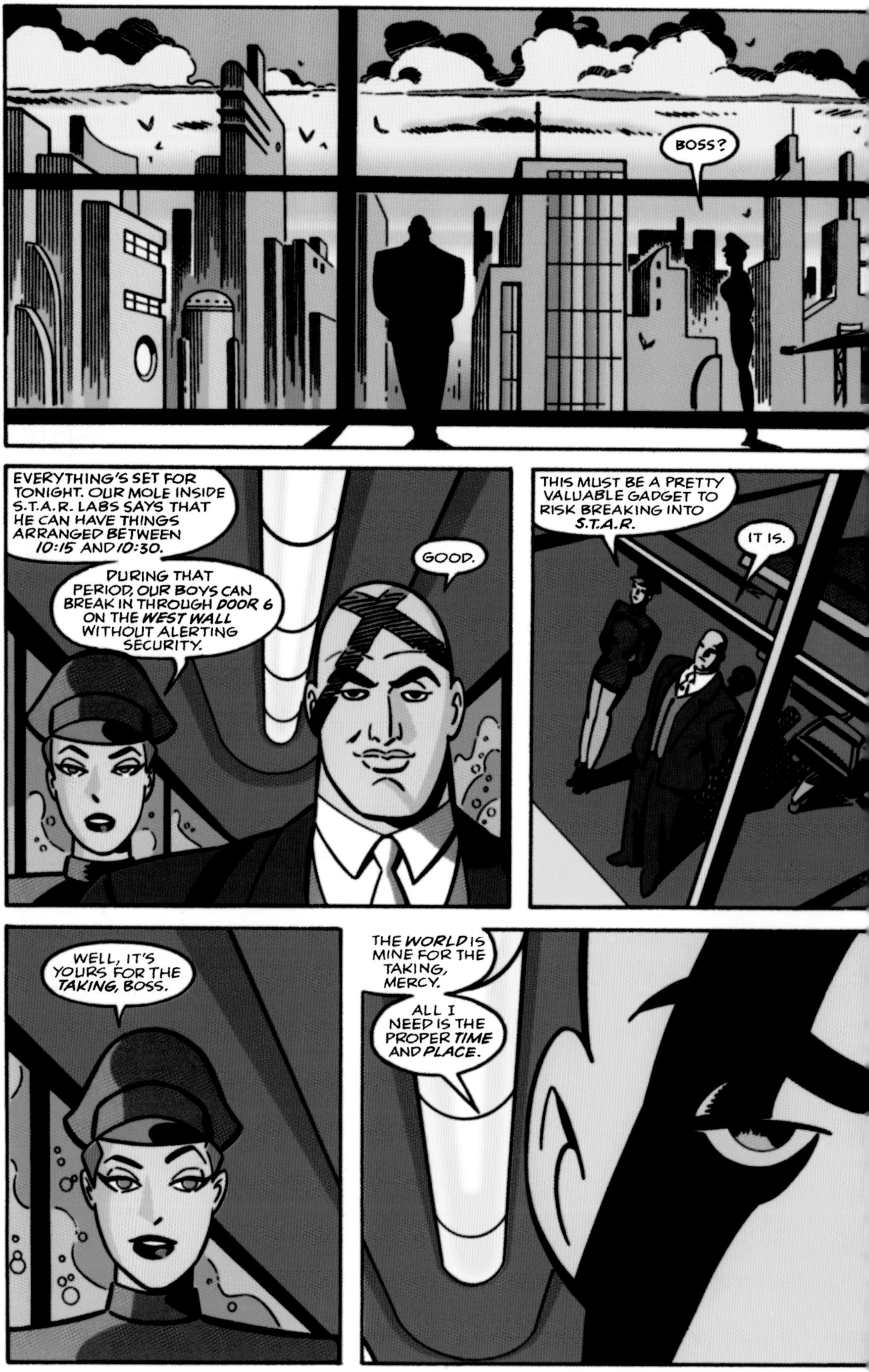
BOSS?
EVERYTHING'S SET FOR TONIGHT. OUR MOLE INSIDE S.T.A.R. LABS SAYS THAT HE CAN HAVE THINGS ARRANGED BETWEEN 10:15 AND 10:30.
DURING THAT PERIOD, OUR BOYS CAN BREAK IN THROUGH DOOR 6 ON THE WEST WALL WITHOUT ALERTING SECURITY.
GOOD.
THIS MUST BE A PRETTY VALUABLE GADGET TO RISK BREAKING INTO S.T.A.R.
IT IS.
WELL, IT'S YOURS FOR THE TAKING, BOSS.
THE WORLD IS MINE FOR THE TAKING, MERCY.
ALL I NEED IS THE PROPER TIME AND PLACE.

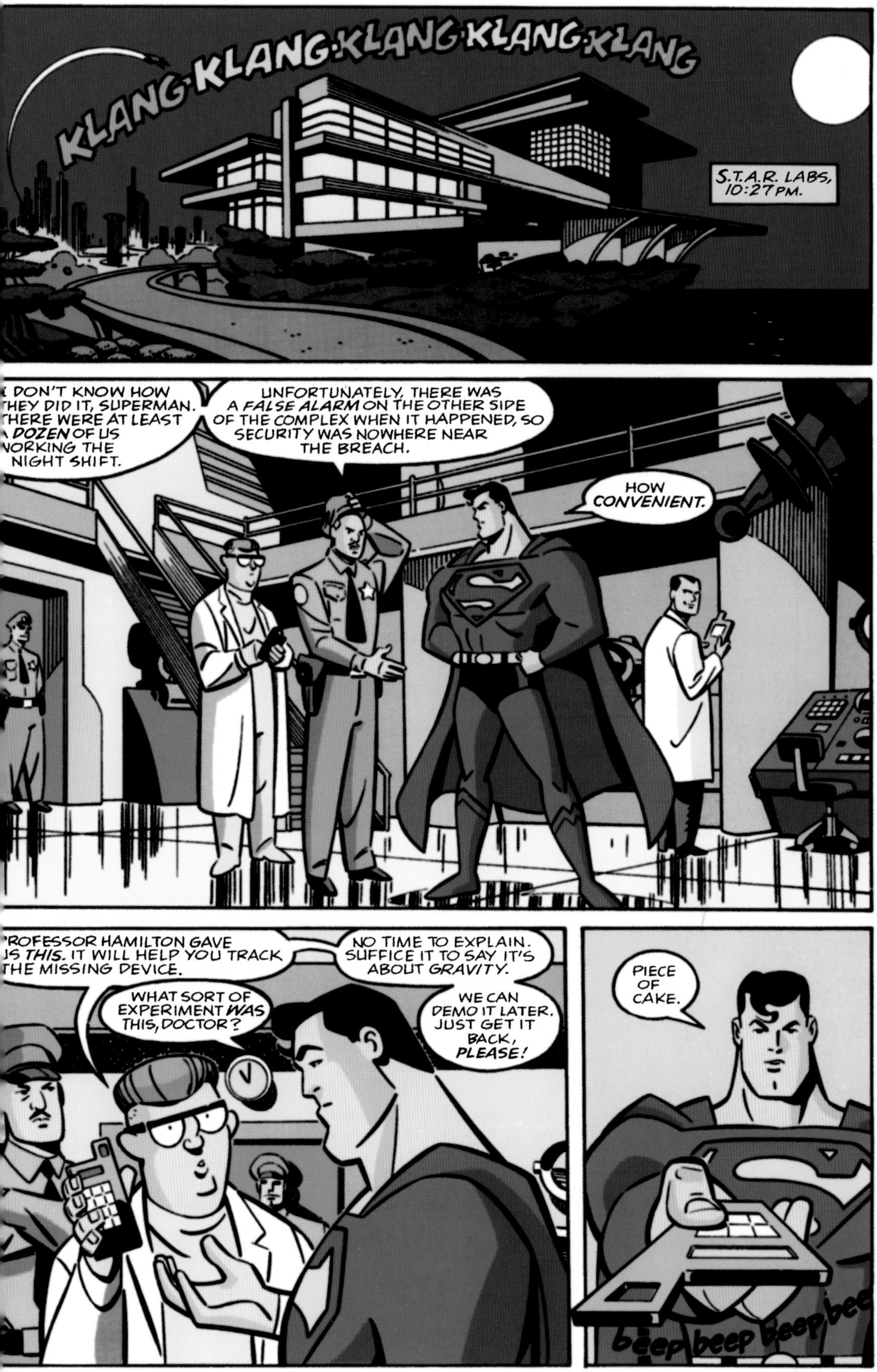
KLANG-KLANG-KLANG-KLANG-KLANG
S.T.A.R. LABS, 10:27 PM.
I DON'T KNOW HOW THEY DID IT, SUPERMAN. THERE WERE AT LEAST A DOZEN OF US WORKING THE NIGHT SHIFT.
UNFORTUNATELY, THERE WAS A FALSE ALARM ON THE OTHER SIDE OF THE COMPLEX WHEN IT HAPPENED, SO SECURITY WAS NOWHERE NEAR THE BREACH.
HOW CONVENIENT.
PROFESSOR HAMILTON GAVE US THIS. IT WILL HELP YOU TRACK THE MISSING DEVICE.
WHAT SORT OF EXPERIMENT WAS THIS, DOCTOR?
NO TIME TO EXPLAIN. SUFFICE IT TO SAY IT'S ABOUT GRAVITY.
WE CAN DEMO IT LATER. JUST GET IT BACK, PLEASE!
PIECE OF CAKE.
beep beep beep bee

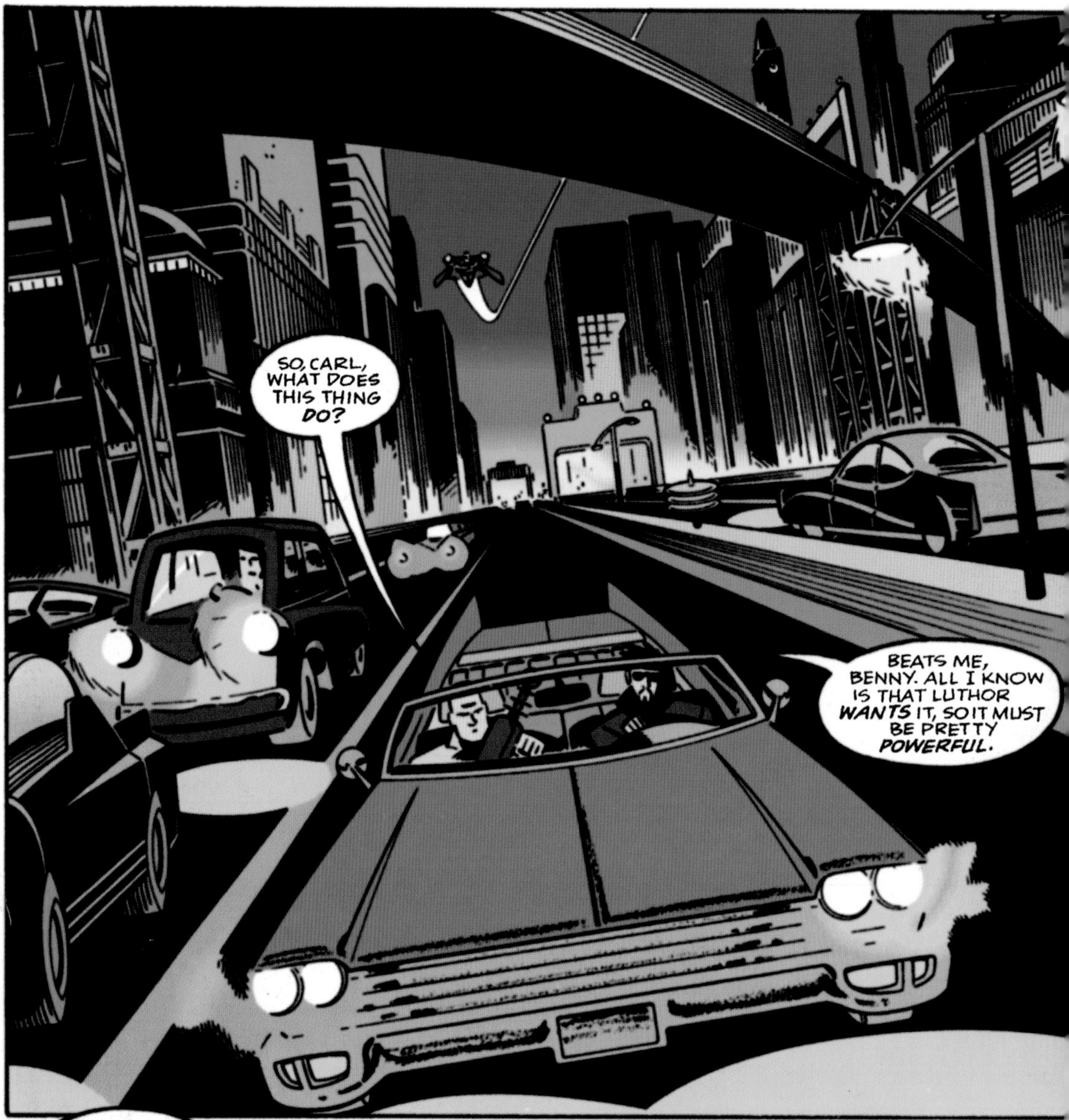
SO, CARL, WHAT DOES THIS THING DO?
BEATS ME, BENNY. ALL I KNOW IS THAT LUTHOR WANTS IT, SO IT MUST BE PRETTY POWERFUL.

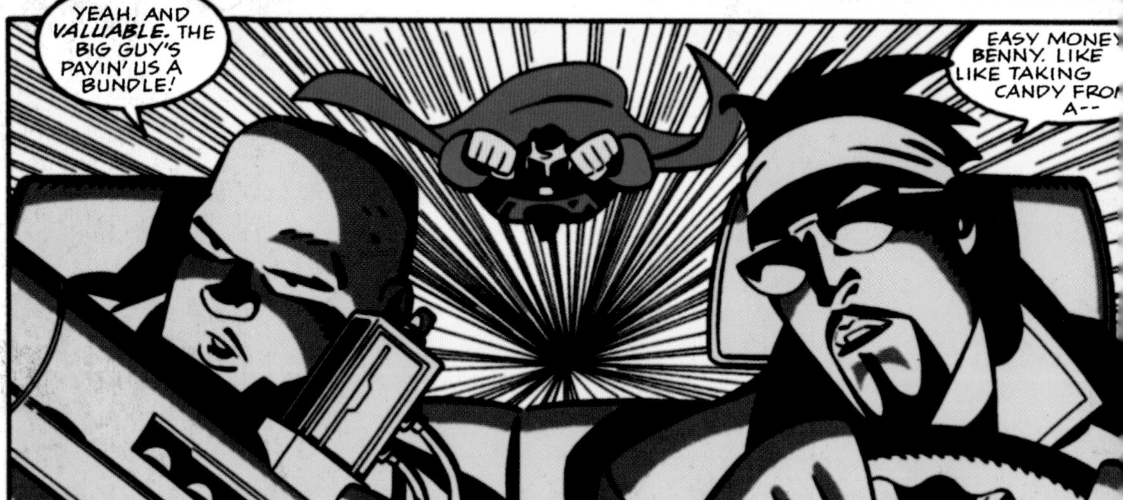
YEAH. AND VALUABLE. THE BIG GUY'S PAYIN' US A BUNDLE!
EASY MONEY BENNY. LIKE LIKE TAKING CANDY FRO A--

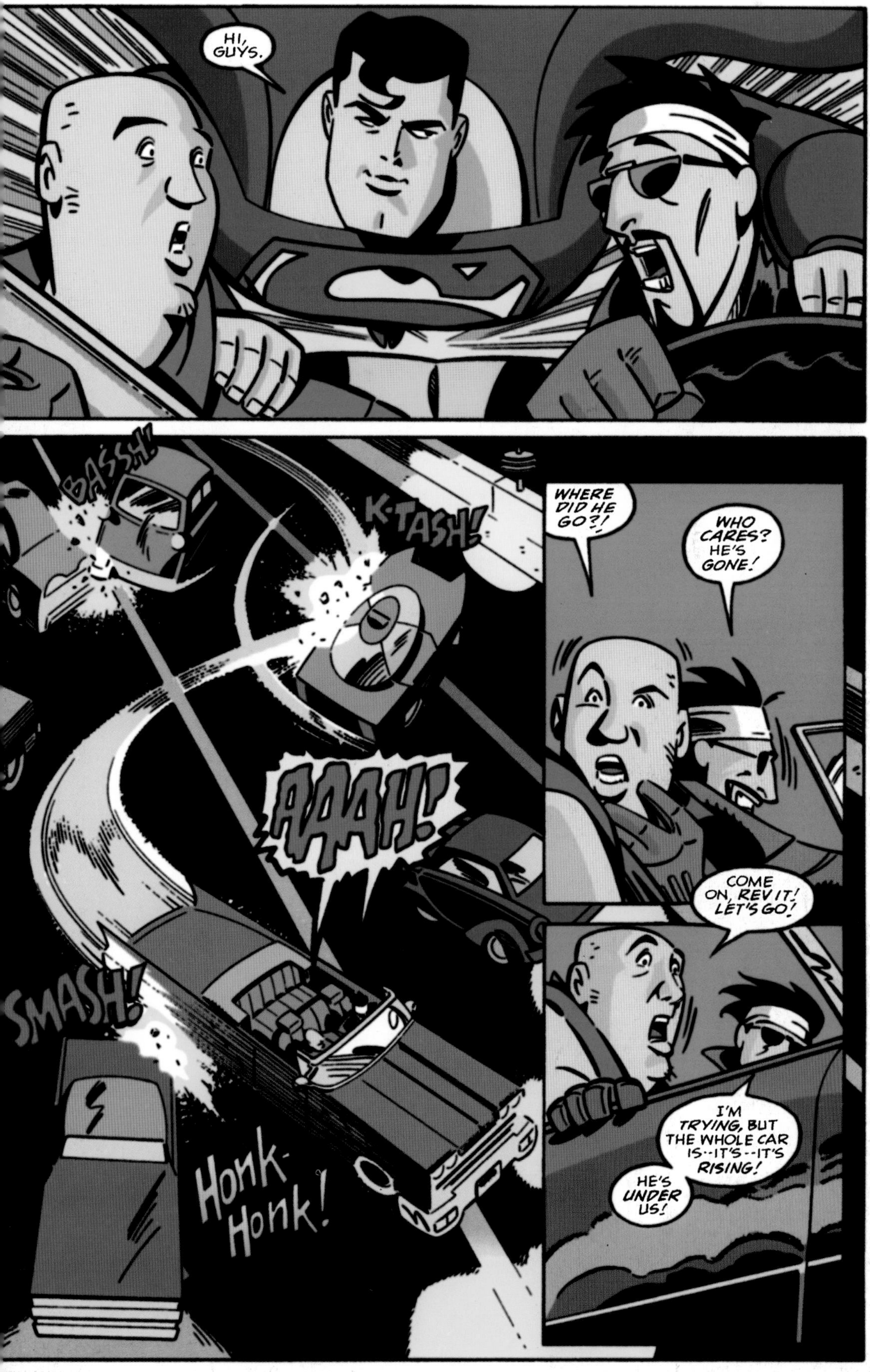
HI, GUYS.
BASSH!
K-TASH!
AAAH!
SMASH!
HONK-HONK!
WHERE DID HE GO?!
WHO CARES? HE'S GONE!
COME ON, REV IT! LET'S GO!
I'M TRYING, BUT THE WHOLE CAR IS--IT'S--IT'S RISING!
HE'S UNDER US!

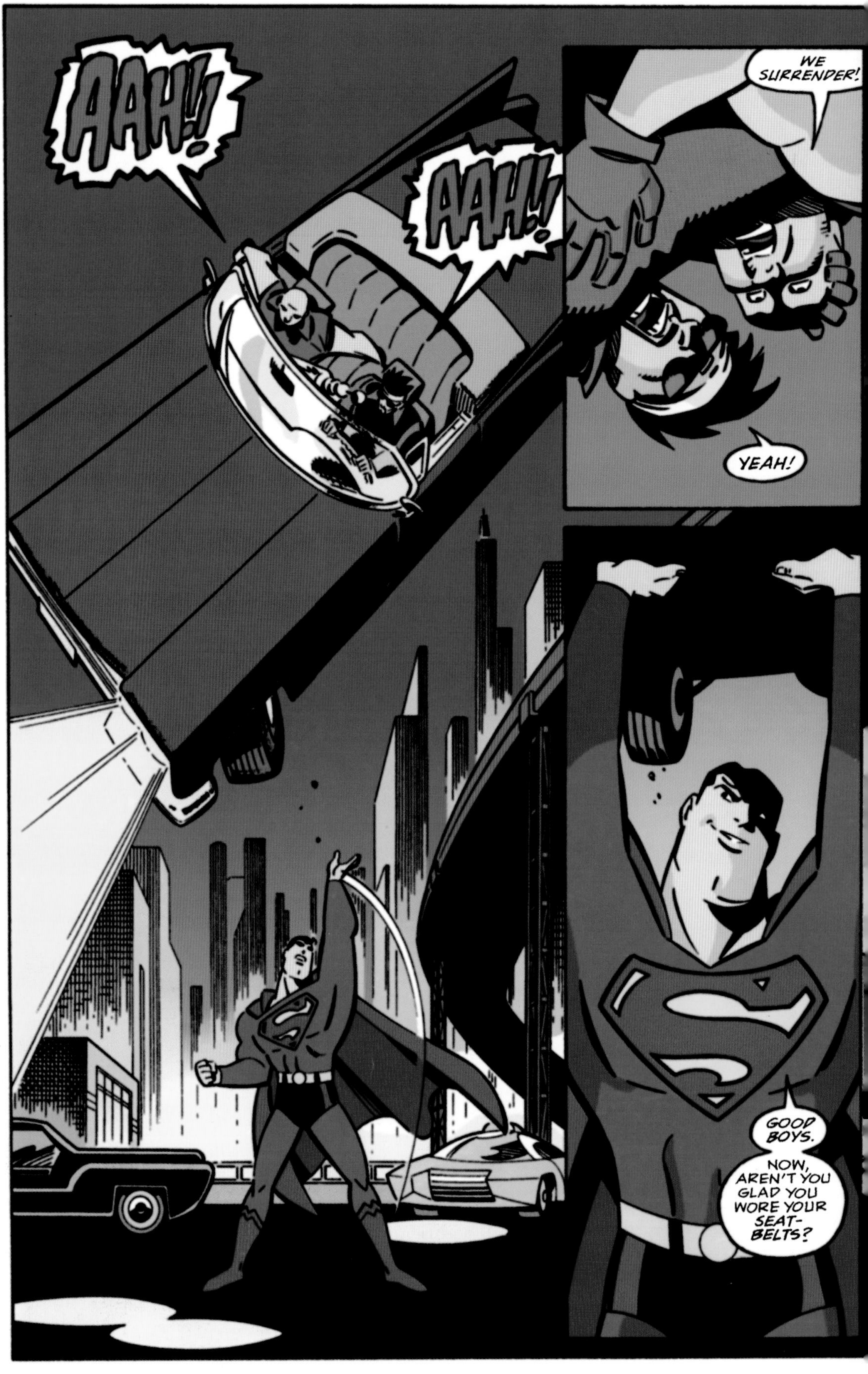
AAH!!
AAH!!
WE SURRENDER!
YEAH!
GOOD BOYS.
NOW, AREN'T YOU GLAD YOU WORE YOUR SEAT-BELTS?

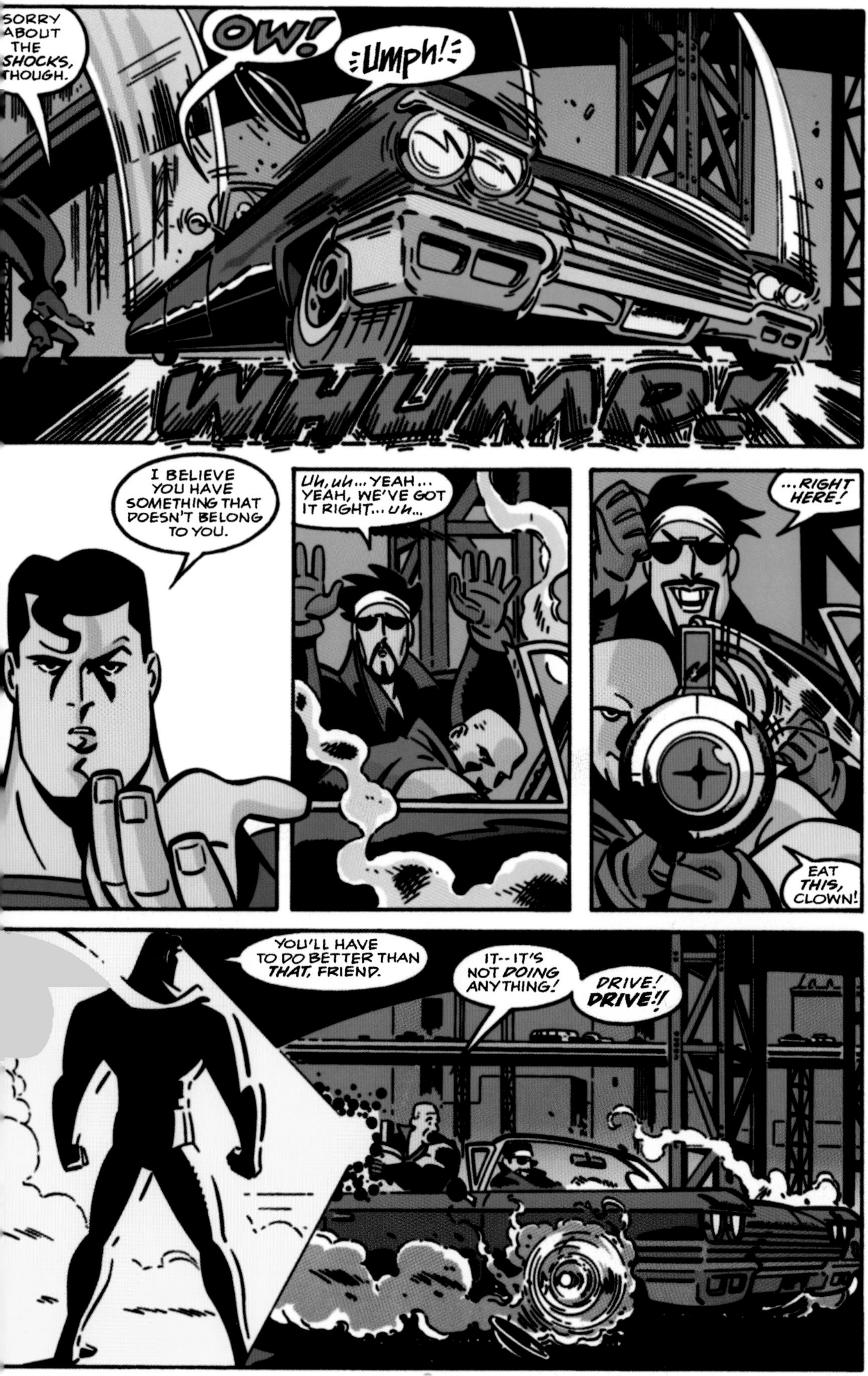

SORRY ABOUT THE SHOCKS, THOUGH.
OW!
Umph!
WHUMP!
I BELIEVE YOU HAVE SOMETHING THAT DOESN'T BELONG TO YOU.
Uh, uh... YEAH... YEAH, WE'VE GOT IT RIGHT... uh...
...RIGHT HERE!
EAT THIS, CLOWN!
YOU'LL HAVE TO DO BETTER THAN THAT, FRIEND.
IT--IT'S NOT DOING ANYTHING!
DRIVE! DRIVE!!

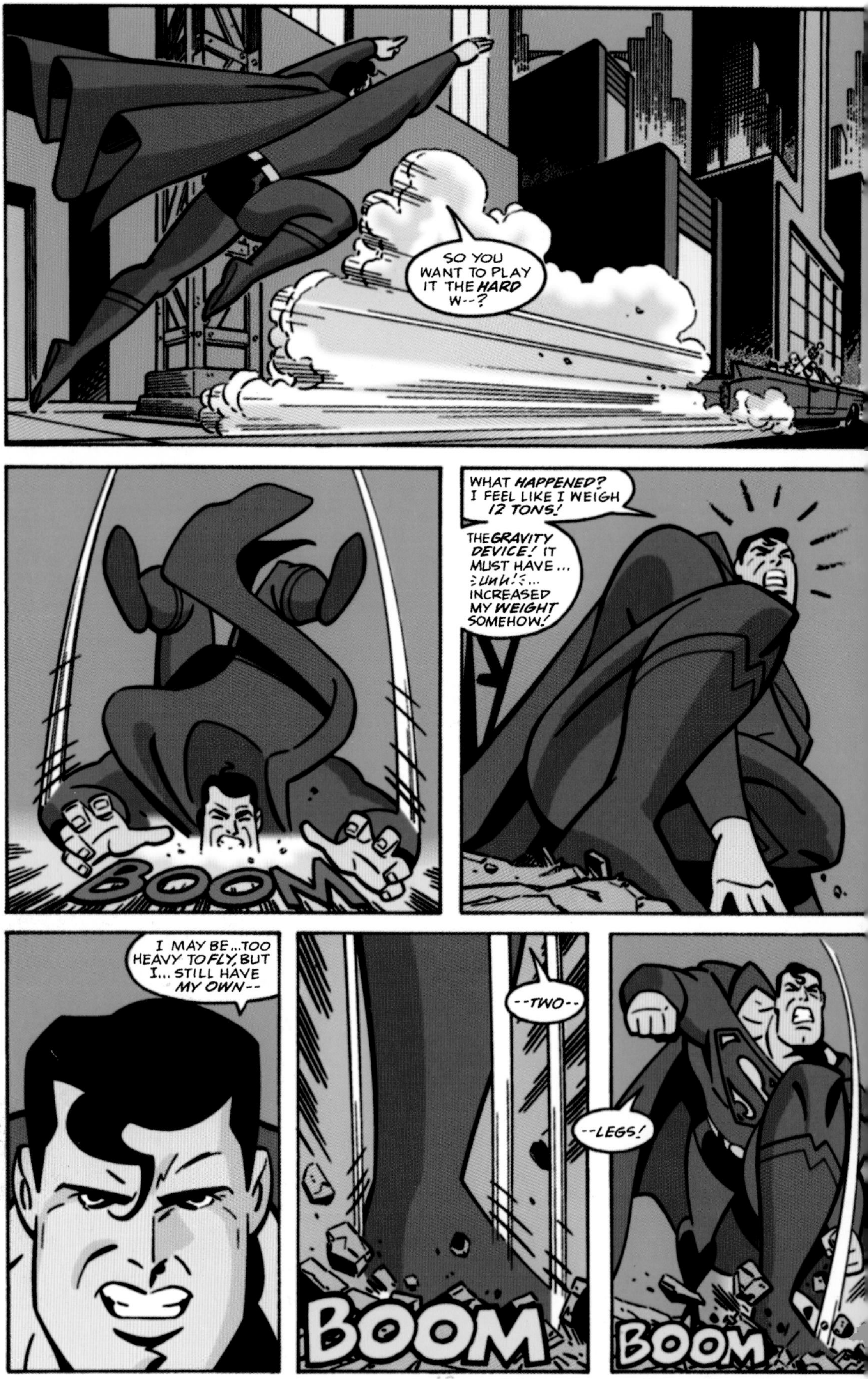
SO YOU WANT TO PLAY IT THE HARD W--?
BOOM
WHAT HAPPENED? I FEEL LIKE I WEIGH 12 TONS!
THE GRAVITY DEVICE! IT MUST HAVE... UNH!... INCREASED MY WEIGHT SOMEHOW!
I MAY BE...TOO HEAVY TO FLY, BUT I... STILL HAVE MY OWN--
--TWO--
BOOM
--LEGS!
BOOM

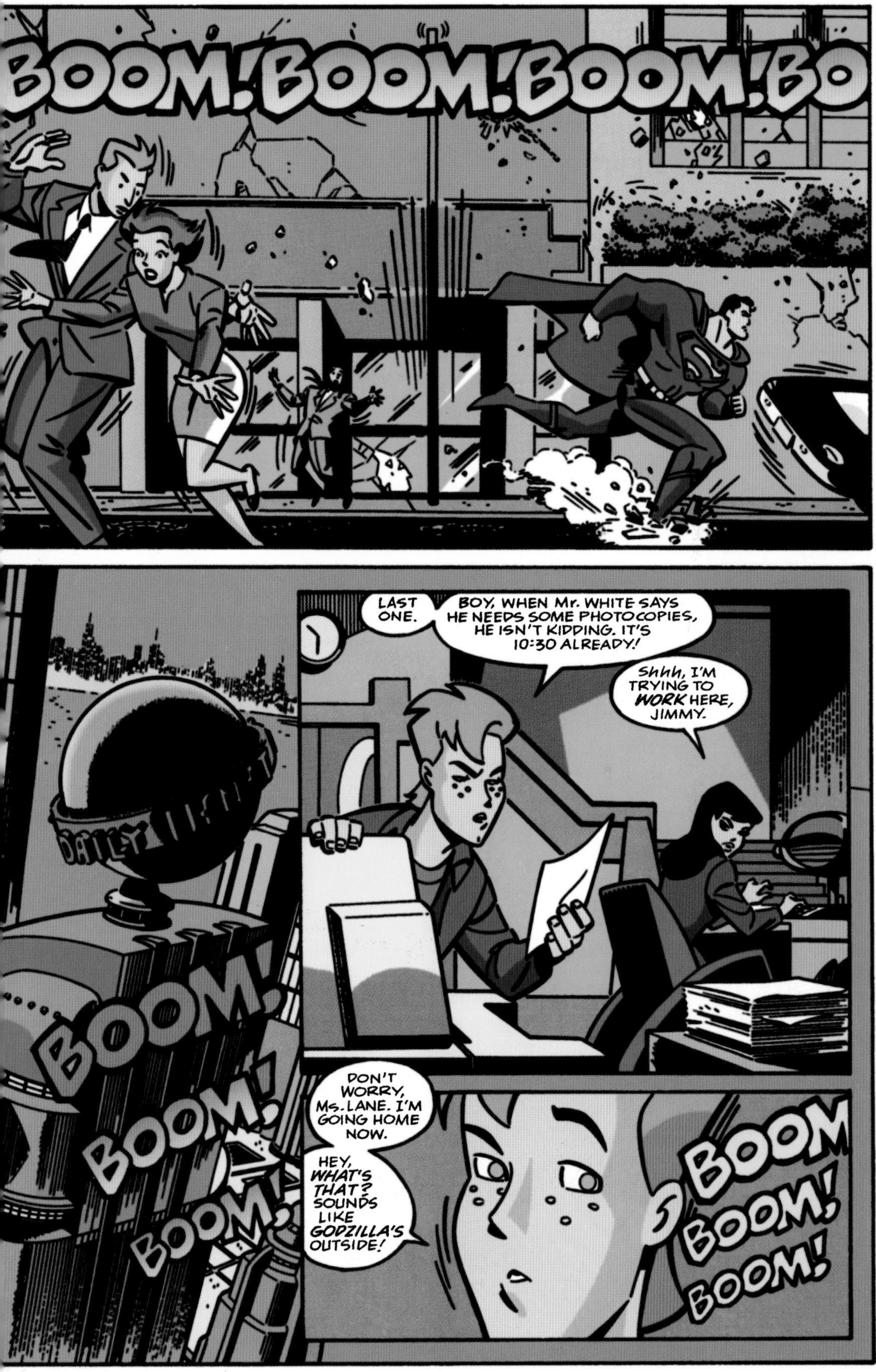
BOOM! BOOM! BOOM! BO
BOOM! BOOM! BOOM!
LAST ONE.
BOY, WHEN Mr. WHITE SAYS HE NEEDS SOME PHOTOCOPIES, HE ISN'T KIDDING. IT'S 10:30 ALREADY!
Shhh, I'M TRYING TO *WORK* HERE, JIMMY.
DON'T WORRY, Ms. LANE. I'M GOING HOME NOW.
HEY, *WHAT'S THAT?* SOUNDS LIKE *GODZILLA'S* OUTSIDE!
BOOM BOOM! BOOM!

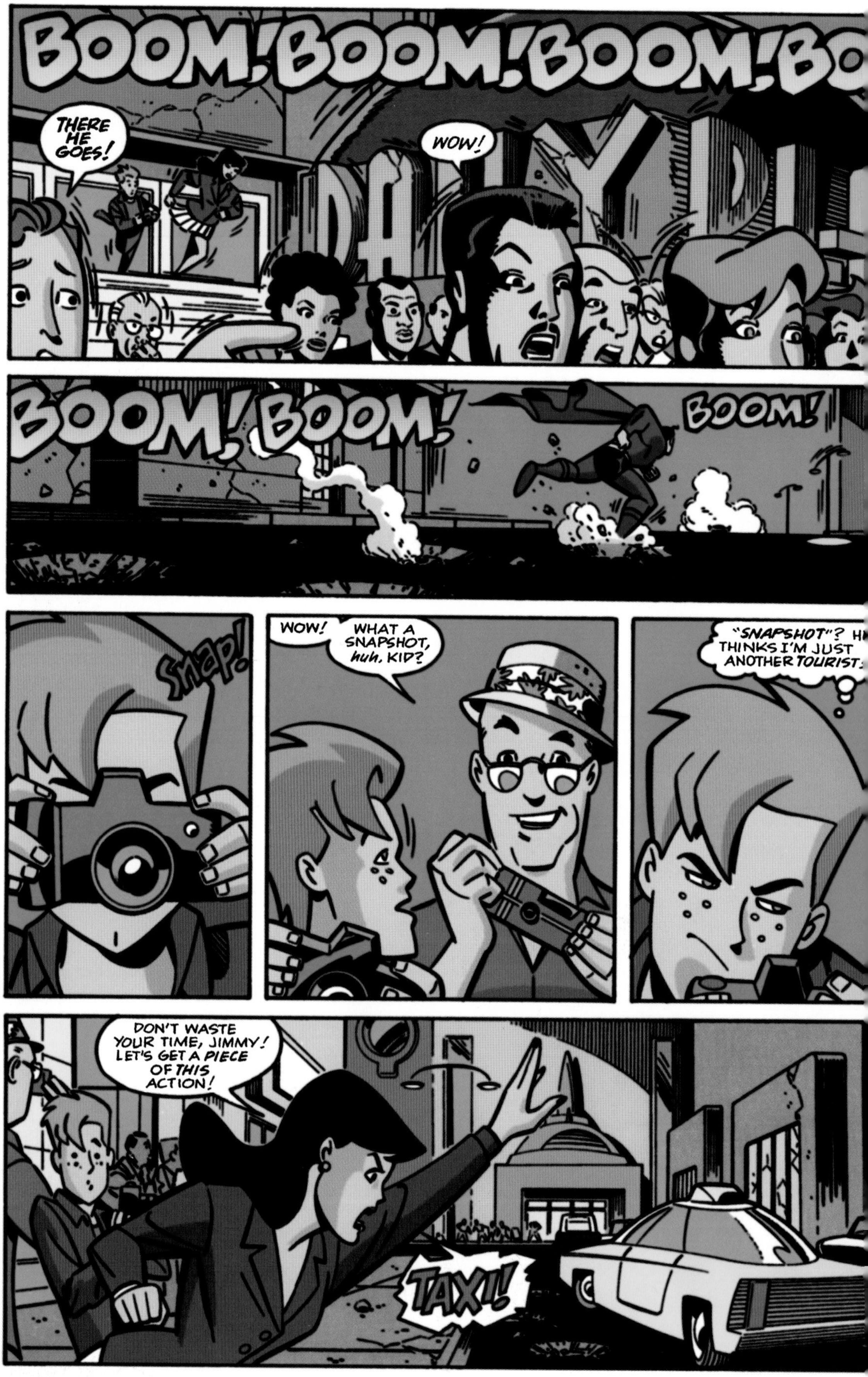

BOOM! BOOM! BOOM!
THERE HE GOES!
WOW!
BOOM! BOOM!
BOOM!
SNAP!
WOW!
WHAT A SNAPSHOT, *huh*, KID?
"*SNAPSHOT*"? H
THINKS I'M JUST ANOTHER *TOURIST*
DON'T WASTE YOUR TIME, JIMMY! LET'S GET A *PIECE* OF *THIS* ACTION!
TAXI!

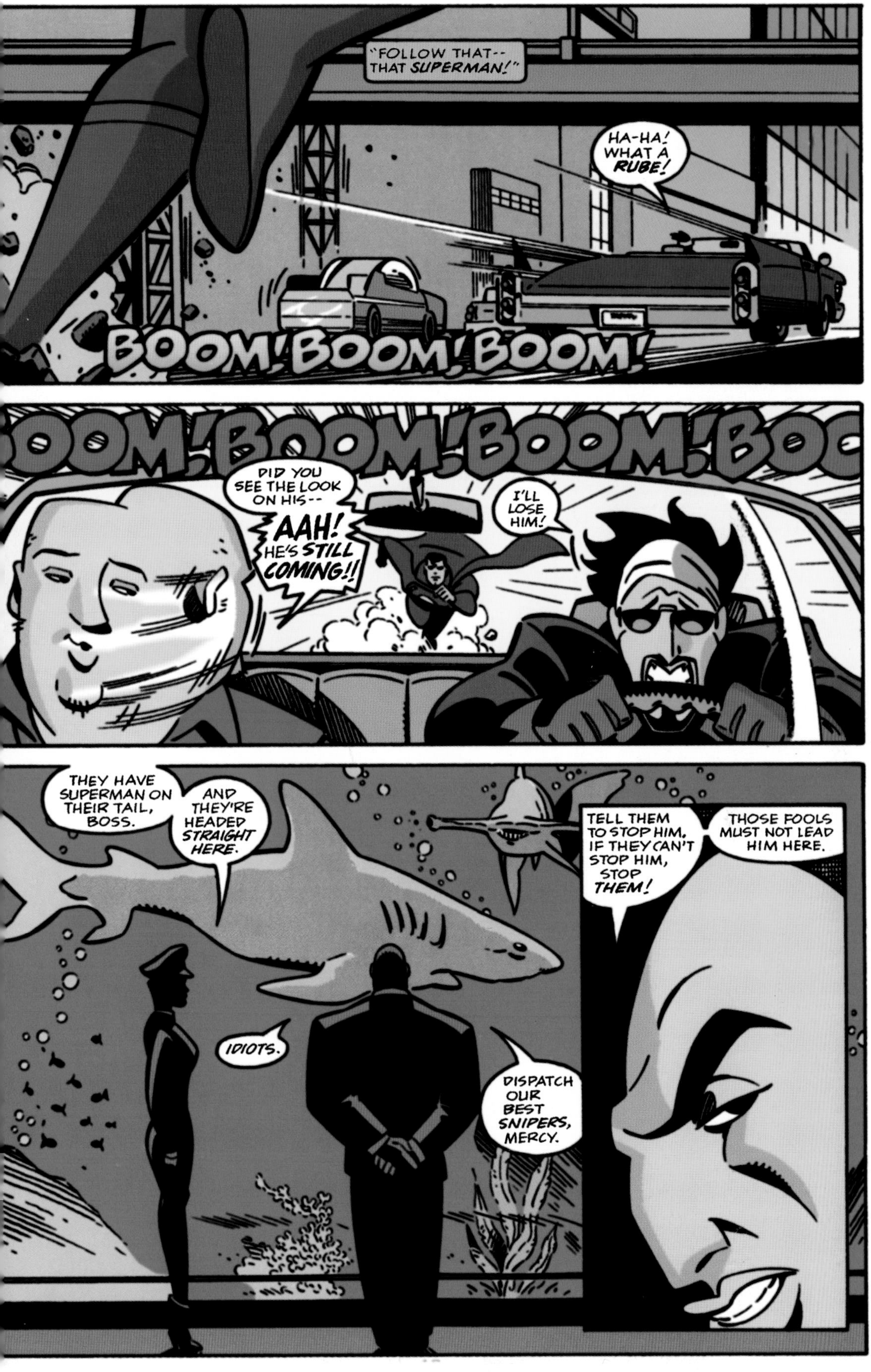
"FOLLOW THAT-- THAT SUPERMAN!"
HA-HA! WHAT A RUBE!
BOOM! BOOM! BOOM!
BOOM! BOOM! BOOM! BOO
DID YOU SEE THE LOOK ON HIS--
AAH! HE'S STILL COMING!!
I'LL LOSE HIM!
THEY HAVE SUPERMAN ON THEIR TAIL, BOSS.
AND THEY'RE HEADED STRAIGHT HERE.
TELL THEM TO STOP HIM. IF THEY CAN'T STOP HIM, STOP THEM!
THOSE FOOLS MUST NOT LEAD HIM HERE.
IDIOTS.
DISPATCH OUR BEST SNIPERS, MERCY.

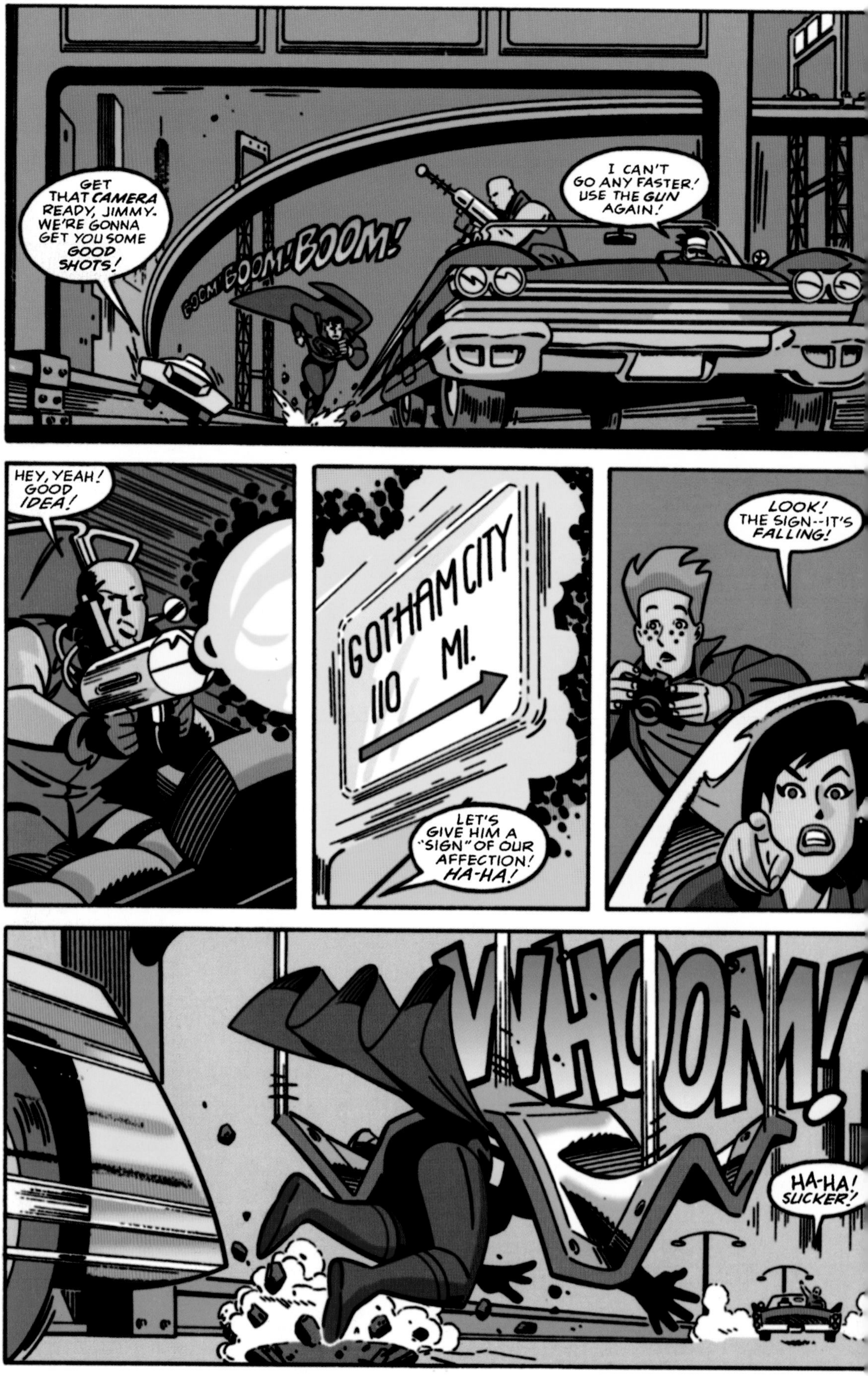

GET THAT CAMERA READY, JIMMY- WE'RE GONNA GET YOU SOME GOOD SHOTS!
BOOM! BOOM! BOOM!
I CAN'T GO ANY FASTER! USE THE GUN AGAIN!
HEY, YEAH! GOOD IDEA!
GOTHAM CITY 110 MI.
LET'S GIVE HIM A "SIGN" OF OUR AFFECTION! HA-HA!
LOOK! THE SIGN--IT'S FALLING!
WHOOM!
HA-HA! SUCKER!

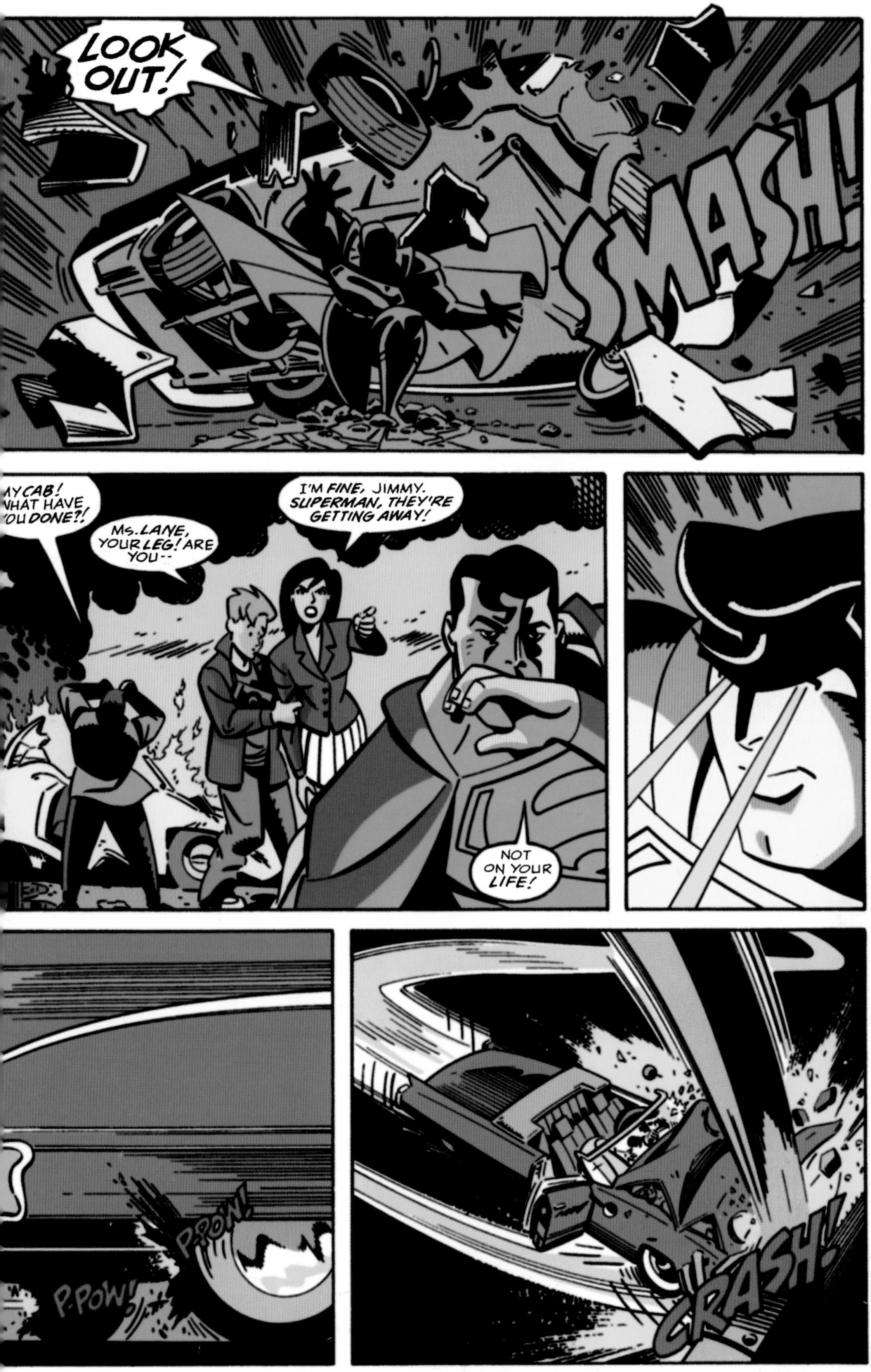
LOOK OUT!
SMASH!!
MY CAB! WHAT HAVE YOU DONE?!
Ms. LANE, YOUR LEG! ARE YOU--
I'M FINE, JIMMY. SUPERMAN, THEY'RE GETTING AWAY!
NOT ON YOUR LIFE!
P-POW!
P-POW!
CRASH!!

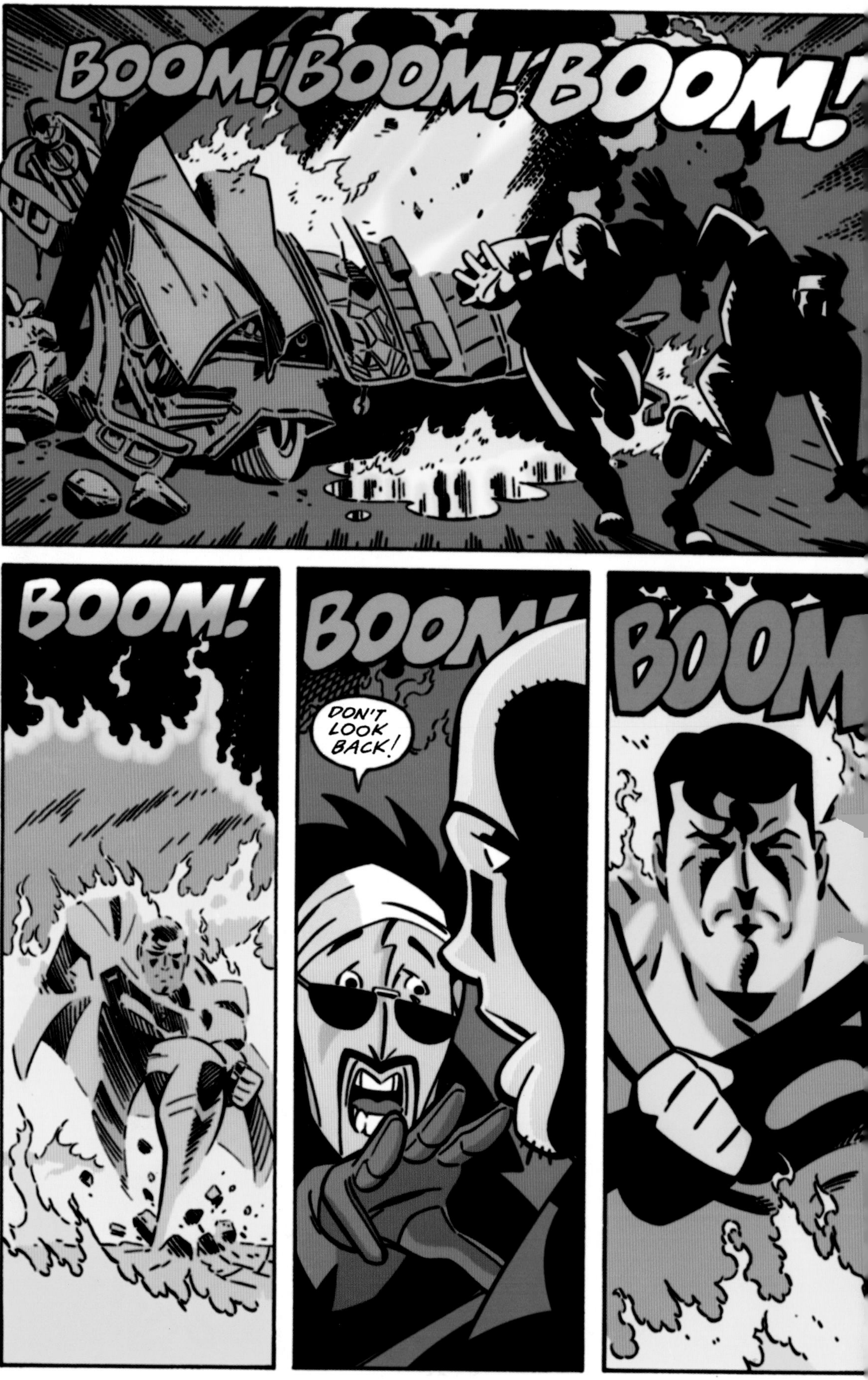
BOOM! BOOM! BOOM!
BOOM!
BOOM!
DON'T LOOK BACK!
BOOM

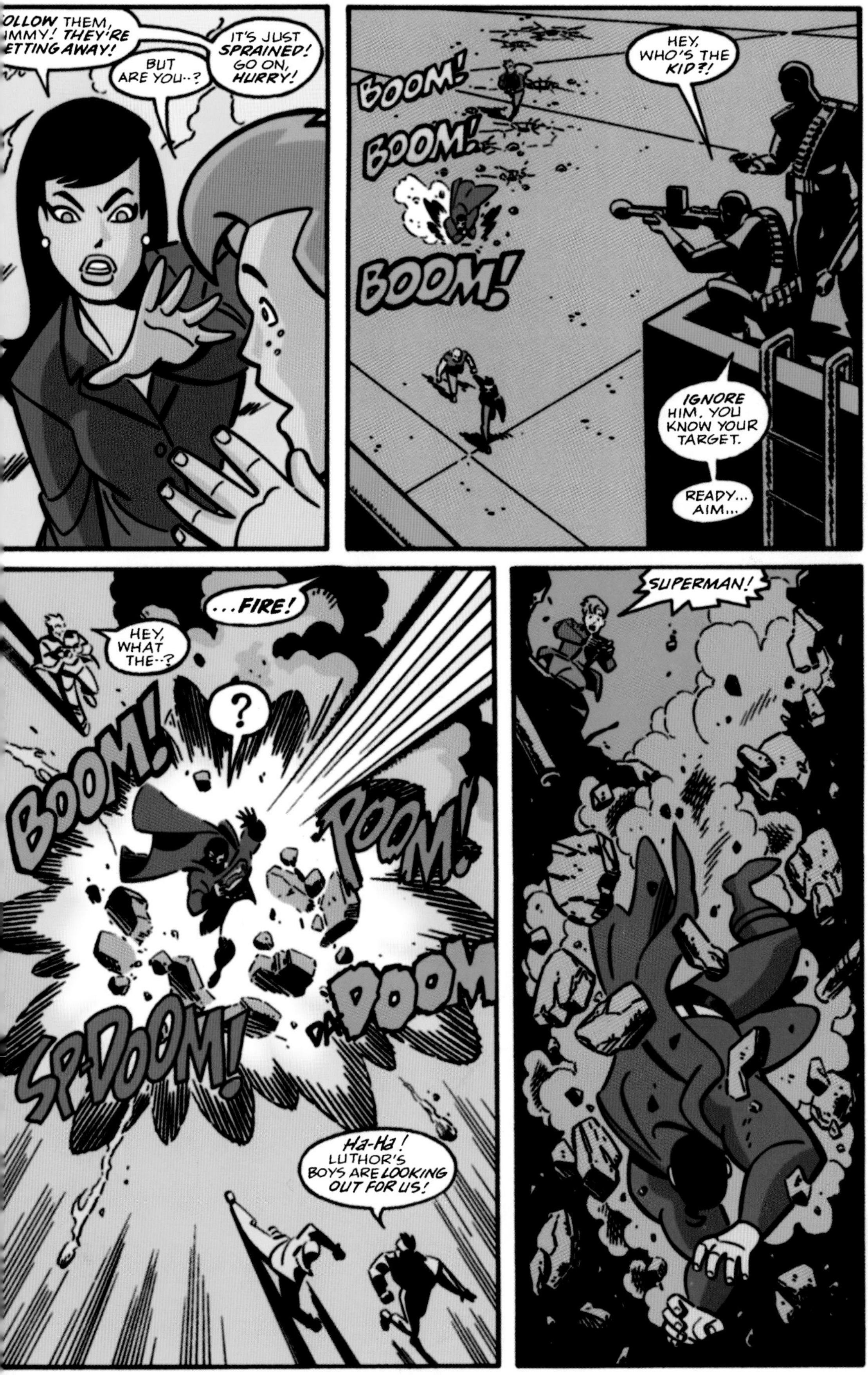

OLLOW THEM, IMMY! THEY'RE ETTING AWAY!
BUT ARE YOU--?
IT'S JUST SPRAINED! GO ON, HURRY!
BOOM!
BOOM!
BOOM!
HEY, WHO'S THE KID?!
IGNORE HIM. YOU KNOW YOUR TARGET.
READY... AIM...
...FIRE!
HEY, WHAT THE--?
?
BOOM!
POOM!
SP-DOOM!
DA-DOOM
Ha-Ha! LUTHOR'S BOYS ARE LOOKING OUT FOR US!
SUPERMAN!

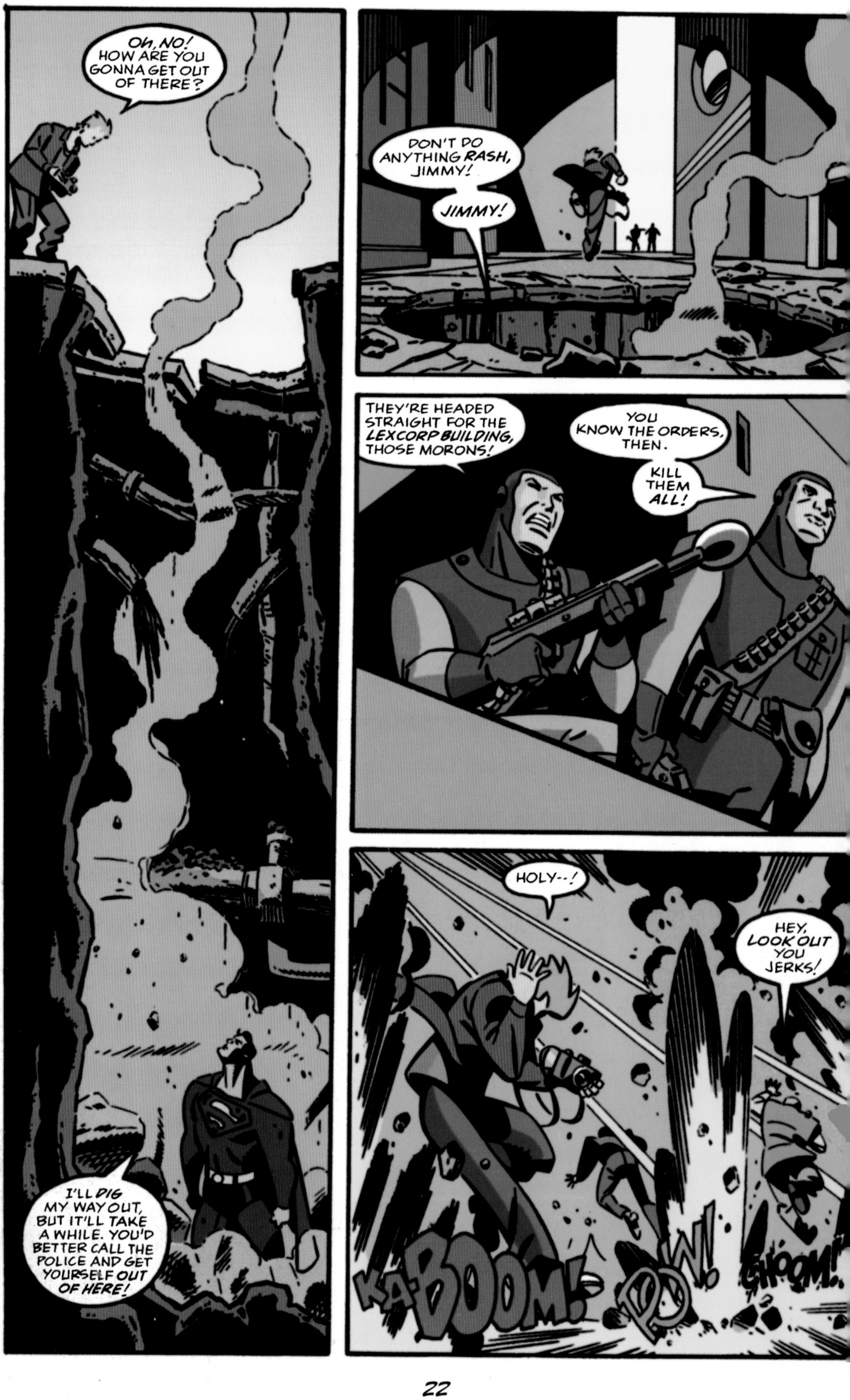

OH, NO! HOW ARE YOU GONNA GET OUT OF THERE?
I'LL DIG MY WAY OUT, BUT IT'LL TAKE A WHILE. YOU'D BETTER CALL THE POLICE AND GET YOURSELF OUT OF HERE!
DON'T DO ANYTHING RASH, JIMMY!
JIMMY!
THEY'RE HEADED STRAIGHT FOR THE LEXCORP BUILDING, THOSE MORONS!
YOU KNOW THE ORDERS, THEN.
KILL THEM ALL!
HOLY--!
HEY, LOOK OUT YOU JERKS!
KA-BOOM!
POW!
CHOOM!

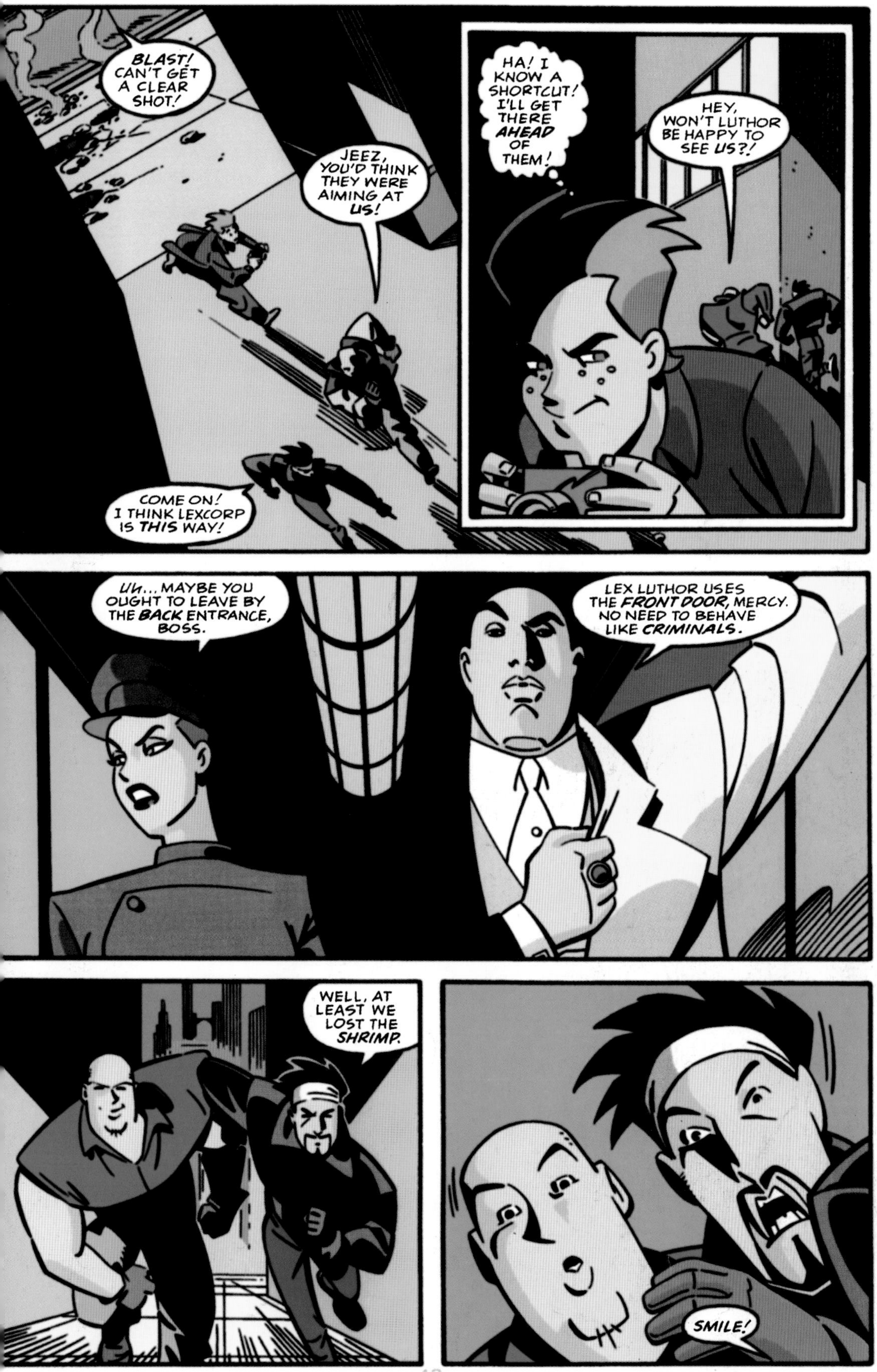
BLAST! CAN'T GET A CLEAR SHOT!
JEEZ, YOU'D THINK THEY WERE AIMING AT US!
COME ON! I THINK LEXCORP IS THIS WAY!
HA! I KNOW A SHORTCUT! I'LL GET THERE AHEAD OF THEM!
HEY, WON'T LUTHOR BE HAPPY TO SEE US?!
UH... MAYBE YOU OUGHT TO LEAVE BY THE BACK ENTRANCE, BOSS.
LEX LUTHOR USES THE FRONT DOOR, MERCY. NO NEED TO BEHAVE LIKE CRIMINALS.
WELL, AT LEAST WE LOST THE SHRIMP.
SMILE!

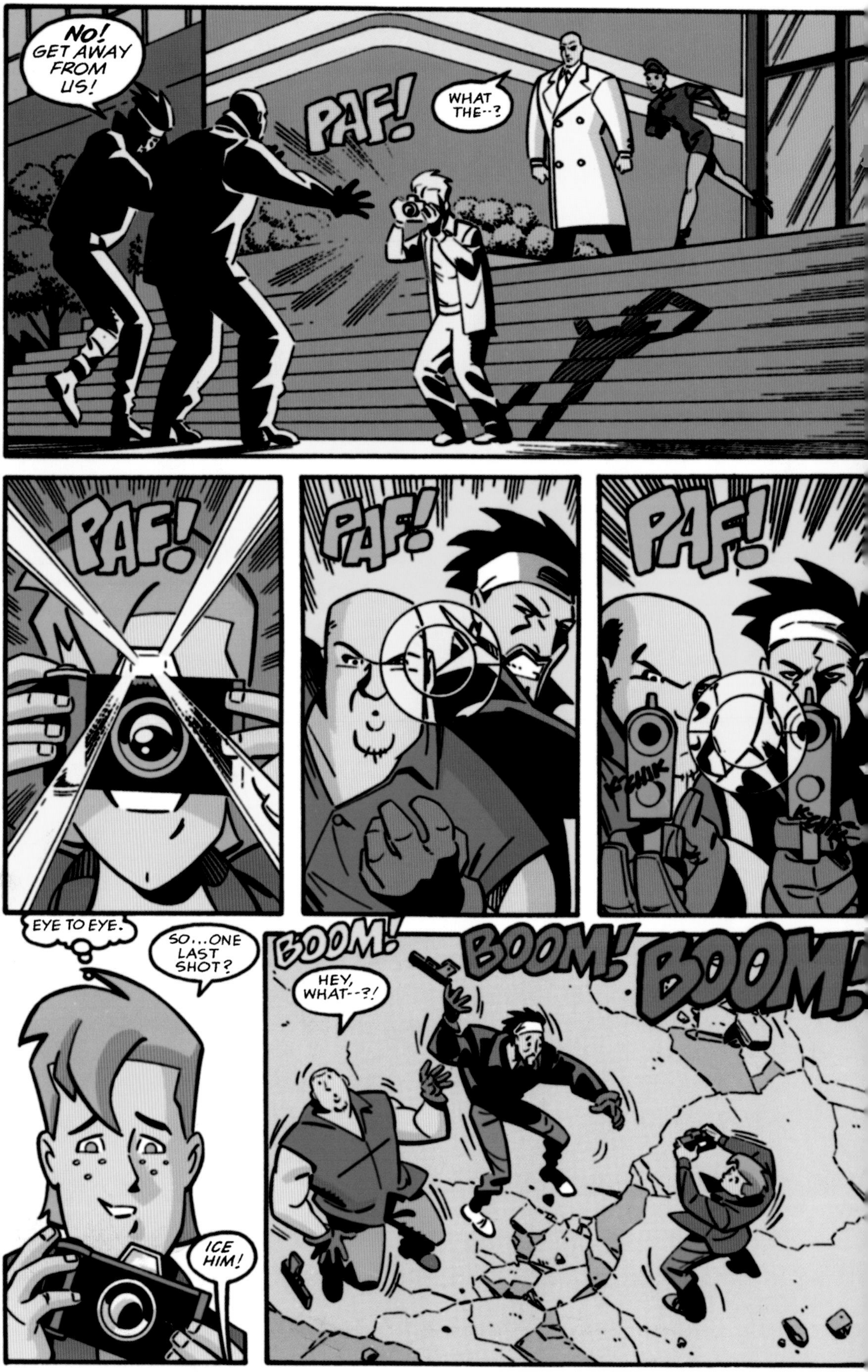
NO! GET AWAY FROM US!
PAF!
WHAT THE--?
PAF!
PAF!
PAF!
K'CHIK
K'CHIK
EYE TO EYE.
SO...ONE LAST SHOT?
ICE HIM!
BOOM!
BOOM!
BOOM!
HEY, WHAT--?!

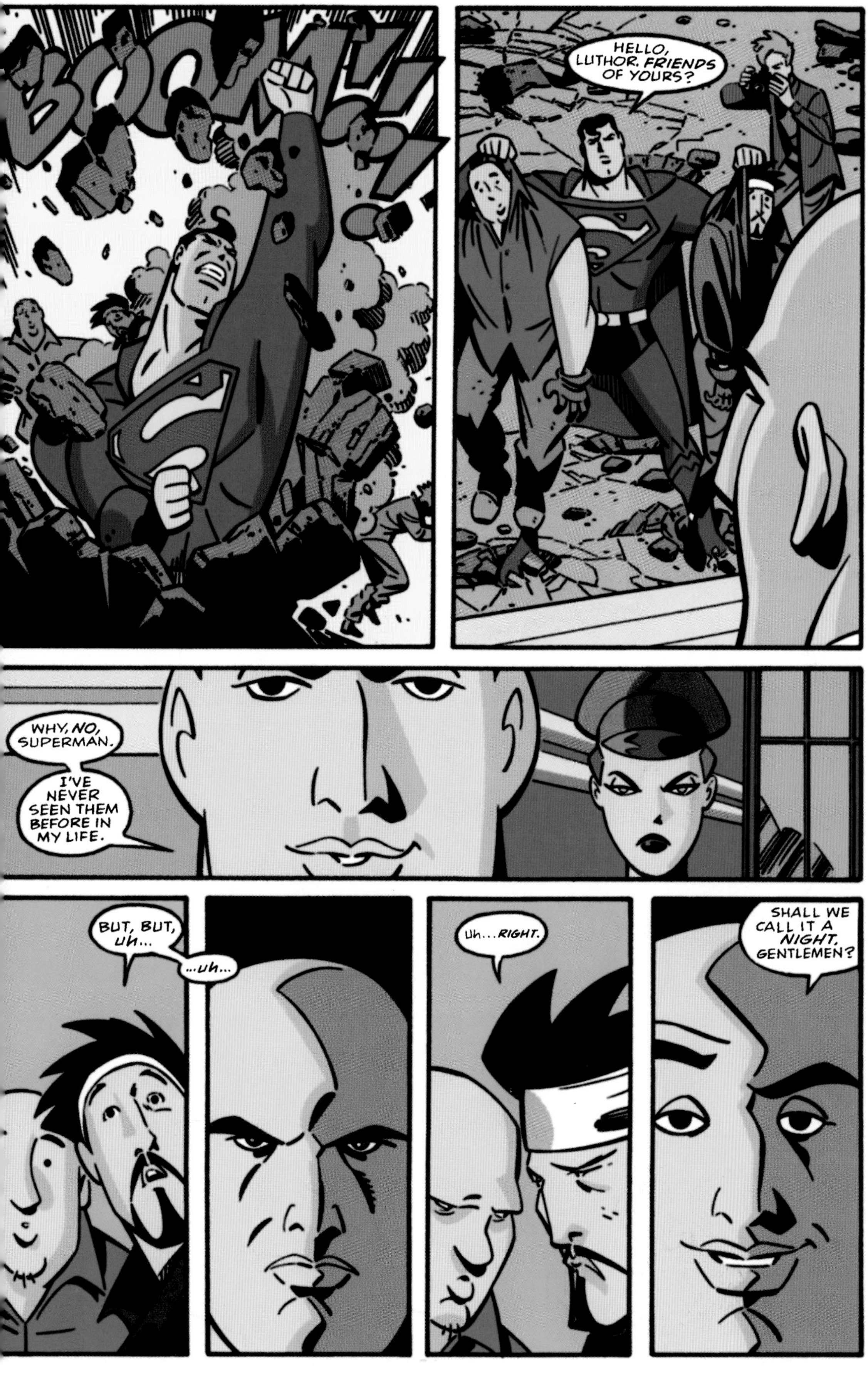
BOOM!!
HELLO, LUTHOR. FRIENDS OF YOURS?
WHY, NO, SUPERMAN.
I'VE NEVER SEEN THEM BEFORE IN MY LIFE.
BUT, BUT, uh...
...uh...
uh... RIGHT.
SHALL WE CALL IT A NIGHT, GENTLEMEN?

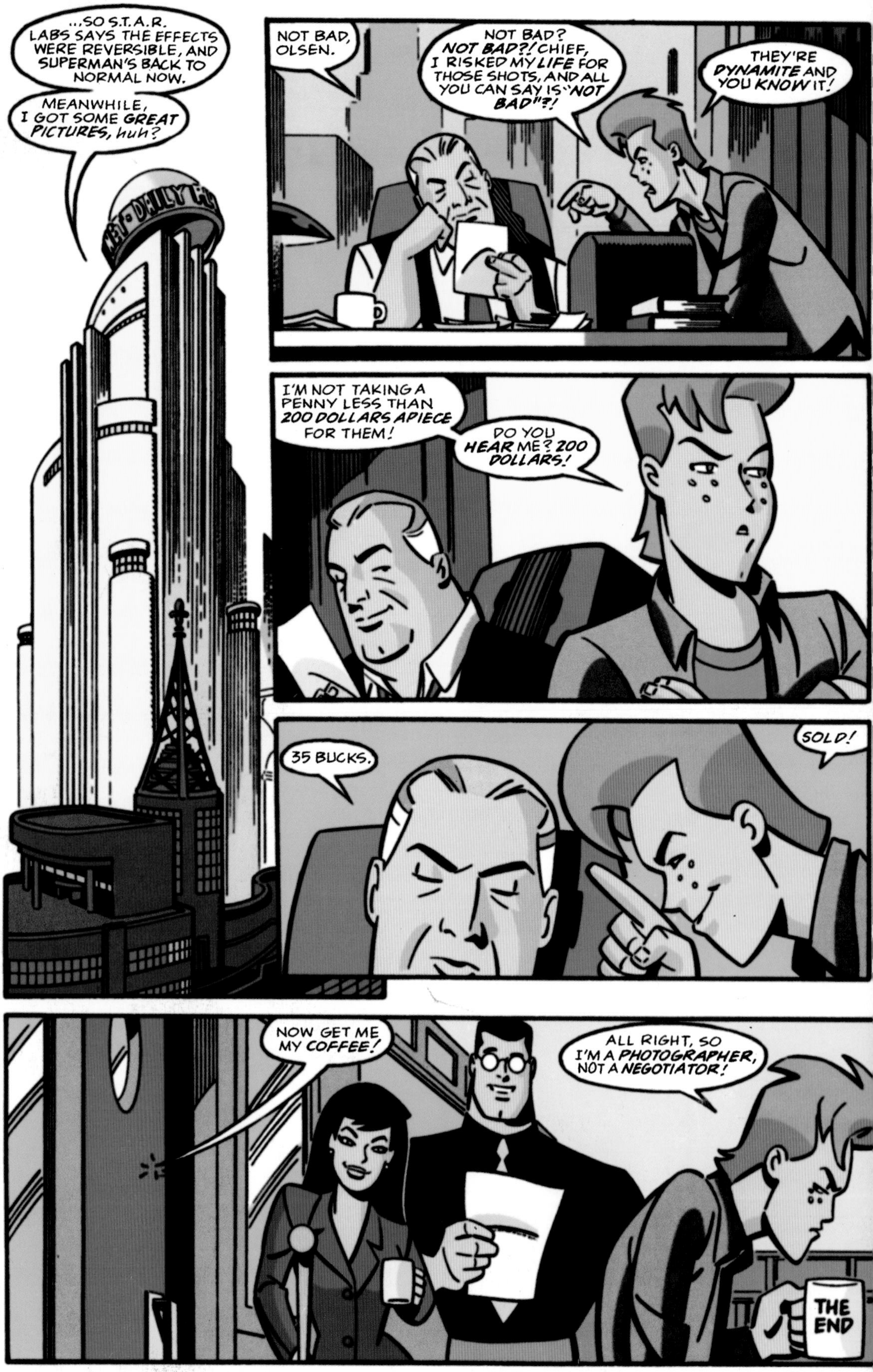
...SO S.T.A.R. LABS SAYS THE EFFECTS WERE REVERSIBLE, AND SUPERMAN'S BACK TO NORMAL NOW.
MEANWHILE, I GOT SOME GREAT PICTURES, huh?
NOT BAD, OLSEN.
NOT BAD? NOT BAD?! CHIEF, I RISKED MY LIFE FOR THOSE SHOTS, AND ALL YOU CAN SAY IS "NOT BAD"?!
THEY'RE DYNAMITE AND YOU KNOW IT!
I'M NOT TAKING A PENNY LESS THAN 200 DOLLARS APIECE FOR THEM!
DO YOU HEAR ME? 200 DOLLARS!
35 BUCKS.
SOLD!
NOW GET ME MY COFFEE!
ALL RIGHT, SO I'M A PHOTOGRAPHER, NOT A NEGOTIATOR!
THE END

CREATORS

SCOTT McCLOUD WRITER

Scott McCloud is an acclaimed comics creator and author whose best-known work is the graphic novel *Understanding Comics*. His work also includes the science-fiction adventure series *Zot!*, a 12-issue run of *Superman Adventures,* and much more. Scott is the creator of the "24 Hour Comic," and frequently lectures on comics theory.

RICK BURCHETT PENCILLER

Rick Burchett has worked as a comics artist for more than 25 years. He has received the comics industry's Eisner Award three times, Spain's Haxtur Award, and he has been nominated for England's Eagle Award. Rick lives with his wife and two sons near St. Louis, Missouri.

TERRY AUSTIN INKER

Throughout his career, inker Terry Austin has received dozens of awards for his work on high-profile comics for DC Comics and Marvel, such as *The Uncanny X-Men*, *Doctor Strange*, *Justice League America*, *Green Lantern*, and *Superman Adventures.* He lives near Poughkeepsie, New York.

HEY, WHAT THE--?
...FIRE!
?
BOOM!
POOM!
SP-DOOM!
DA-DOOM
SUPERMAN!

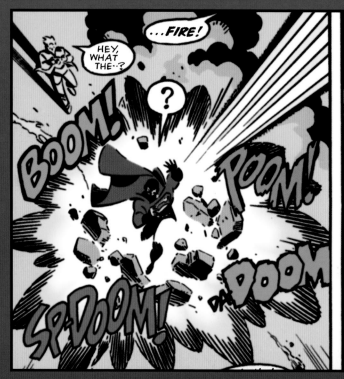

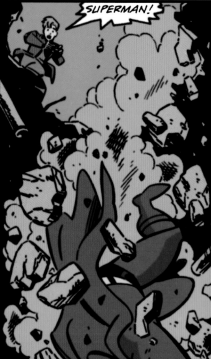

GLOSSARY

affection (uh-FEK-shuhn)--a great liking for someone or something

arranged (uh-RAYJND)--made plans for something to happen

breach (BREECH)--to break through something or make a hole in something

complex (KOM-plex)--a building or group of buildings housing related units

convenient (kuhn-VEE-nyuhnt)--if something is convenient, it is useful or easy to use

coward (KOW-urd)--someone who is easily scared and runs away from frightening situations

dispatch (diss-PACH)--to send something or somebody off

mechanical (muh-KAN-uh-kuhl)--to do with machines or tools, or operated by machinery

negotiator (ni-GOH-shee-ay-tor)--someone who bargains or discusses something so that two parties can come to an agreement

Polaroid (POHL-uh-royd)--a brand of camera that produces developed pictures

reversible (ri-VUR-suh-buhl)--if something is reversible, it is able to be returned to its original condition

surrender (suh-REN-dur)--to give up, or admit that you are beaten

vulnerable (VUHL-nur-uh-buhl)--able to be damaged

SUPERMAN GLOSSARY

Clark Kent: Superman's alter ego, Clark Kent, is a reporter for the *Daily Planet* newspaper and was raised by Ma and Pa Kent. No one knows he is Superman except for his adopted parents, the Kents.

The Daily Planet: the city of Metropolis's biggest and most read newspaper. Clark, Lois, Jimmy, and Perry all work for the *Daily Planet*.

Invulnerability: Superman's invulnerability makes him impervious to harm. Almost nothing can hurt him -- except for Kryptonite, a radioactive rock from his home planet, Krypton.

Jimmy Olsen: Jimmy is a cub reporter and photographer. He is also a friend to Lois and Clark.

Lex Luthor: Lex believes Superman is a threat to Earth and must be stopped. He will do anything it takes to bring the Man of Steel to his knees.

Lois Lane: like Clark Kent, Lois is a reporter at the *Daily Planet* newspaper. She is also one of Clark's best friends.

Metropolis: the city where Clark Kent (Superman) lives.

S.T.A.R. Labs: a research center in Metropolis, where scientists make high-tech tools and devices for Superman and other heroes.

VISUAL QUESTIONS & PROMPTS

1. Why do these two crooks change their minds? What reasons would they have for lying about working for Lex?

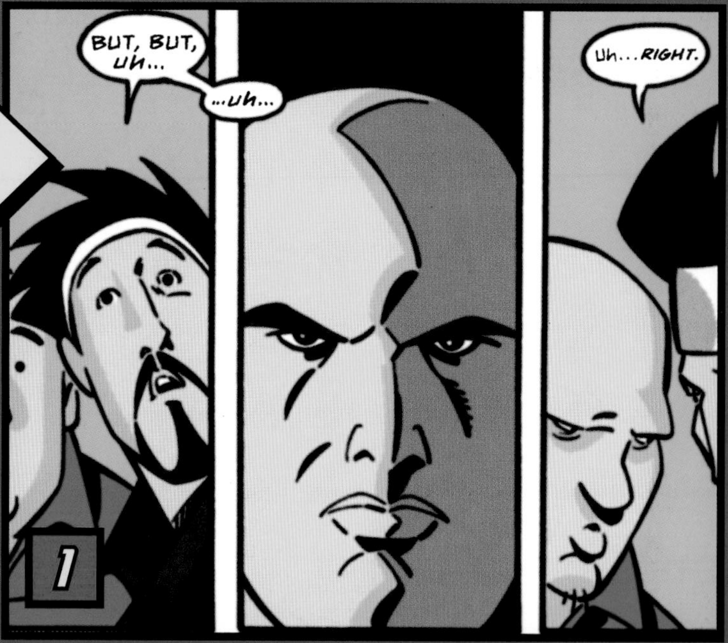
BUT, BUT, UH...
...UH...
UH... RIGHT.
1

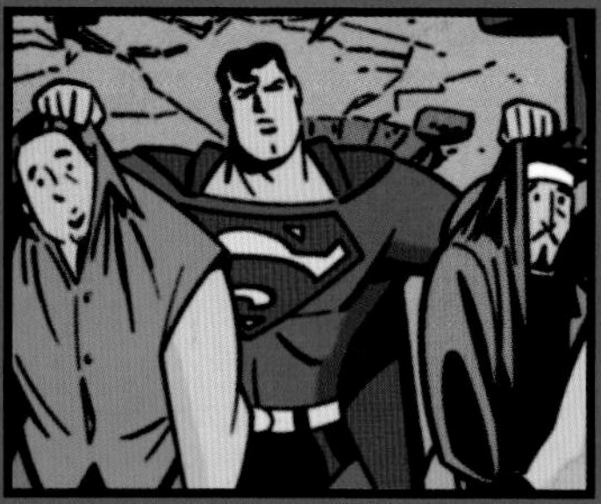

2. Superman uses several of his superpowers in this story as seen in the panel below. Identify three other panels in which Superman uses one of his superpowers.

3. Why would Lex not want the criminals to come to LexCorp? Why might that be bad for him?

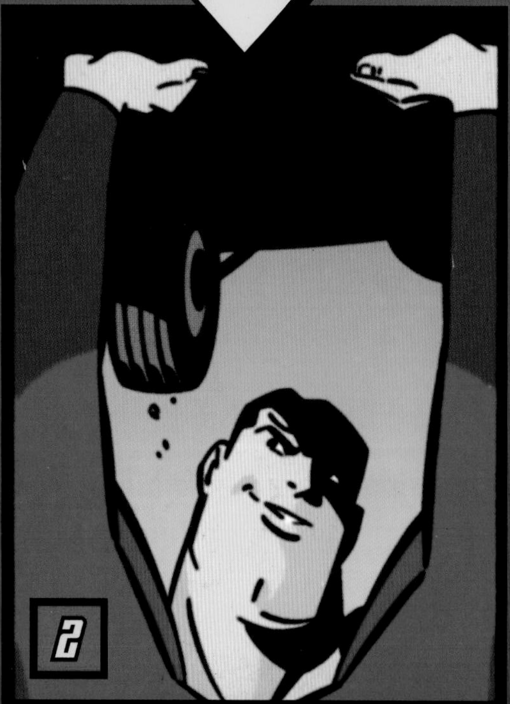
2

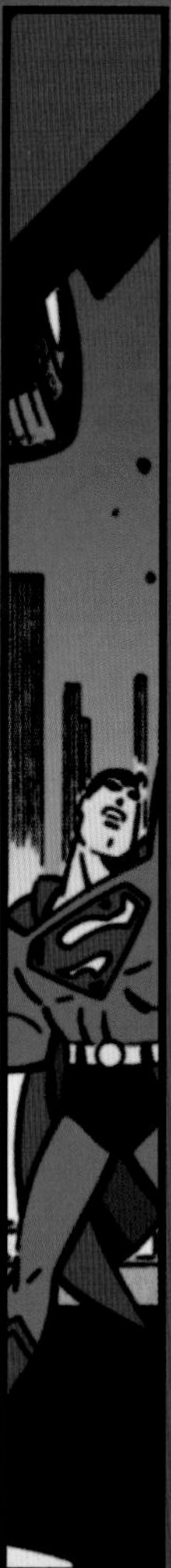

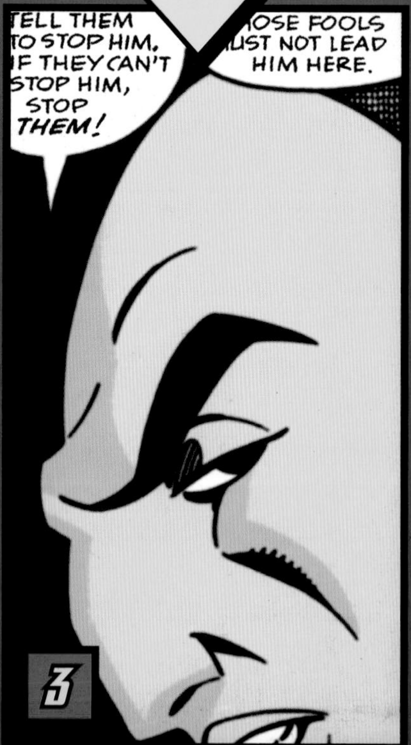
ELL THEM O STOP HIM, F THEY CAN'T STOP HIM, STOP THEM!
OSE FOOLS UST NOT LEAD HIM HERE.
3

4 In the panel below, what does Superman mean by saying the false alarm and security breach happening at the same time was convenient? Explain your answer.

I DON'T KNOW HOW THEY DID IT, SUPERMAN. THERE WERE AT LEAST A *DOZEN* OF US WORKING THE NIGHT SHIFT.

UNFORTUNATELY, THERE WAS A *FALSE ALARM* ON THE OTHER SIDE OF THE COMPLEX WHEN IT HAPPENED, SO SECURITY WAS NOWHERE NEAR THE BREACH.

HOW *CONVENIENT.*

4

VE U TRACK

RT OF NT *WAS* R?

S.T.A.R. LABS, 10:27 PM.

5 Of all the characters in this comic book, who do you think was the most brave and the least brave? Why?

HE'S PROBABLY RIGHT. I WISH I WAS MORE LIKE SUPERMAN.

WELL... I'D HARDLY CALL SUPERMAN *BRAVE.*

WHEN YOU'RE AS STRONG AS SUPERMAN, YOU DON'T *HAVE* TO BE BRAVE.

I'M *FINE*, JIMMY. SUPERMAN, THEY'RE *GETTING AWAY!*

E, 'ARE

PAF!

PAF!

5

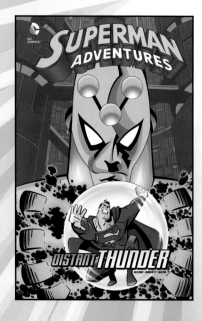

only from...